MW01254822

THE LEGEND OF LEVY

Edited and designed by Douglas King
Copy edited by Jessica Manley

First Printing, December 2020. Printed in the U.S.A.
ISBN: 978-1-7350083-7-0

Artists and galleries interested in receiving entry information for the next Art Folio competition can visit artfolioannual.com for details.

Cover illustration: J. Schuh
Illustrations: Douglas King

First published in the United States of America in 2020 by

Day III Productions, Inc.
www.DayIIIProd.com

THE LEGEND OF LEVY

BRYAN GIBBS

CHAPTER 1

Hot, tired, dirty, and thirsty is about all you could say about my summer. Walking behind Jim's sweaty ass filled my days, and to add insult to injury I did it in my sleep. Jim was my family's prize possession. He was about a sixteen-one-hand mule that could pull a stump from the ground or break a harness trying.

The day seemed hotter than yesterday and working the hard, black dirt seemed impossible, but Jim didn't mind. I was cursing my life, and Jim, when I saw my mother coming up the trail from the house. She was wearing her faded blue dress and carrying a bucket of water and a basket.

"Lunchtime!" she yelled.

I pulled Jim up, unhitched him, took him over to let him rest in the shade, and greeted my mother with a kiss. I plopped down on a large stump that was too much for Jim to pull out of the ground and watched my mom submerge a glass into the bucket of clear water and hand it to me. I gulped it down and dipped the glass back in the bucket, just as my mother reminded me to save some for Jim. Before I could even think, I said, "Screw that damn mule."

My mother slapped me. It stung a bit on my cheek and a tear formed in my eye. My mother said, "I'm sorry for hitting you, Levy, but you mustn't use language like that in front of me or any other lady."

I was embarrassed and ashamed of myself for saying such vulgar things in front of my sweet mother. I wiped the tears from my eyes and told her I was sorry. Truth be told the tears were coming from deeper than the sting of the slap. I guess I was ahead of my brother—I was fifteen years old, and that was the first time I had ever been disciplined by my mom. I had seen her take switches and even a set of bridle leather to my younger brother, but he was wild and mostly a disobedient son. I worked hard every day and outworked my dad and brother most days.

"What's for lunch?" I asked, already knowing the answer.

My mom smiled and hugged me and said, "Leftover venison stew." She handed me the bowl, and I slurped it down and cleaned my bowl with a large slice of mom's bread. I told her thank you as she walked back up the trail towards the cabin we called home.

Mom stopped, smiled, and said, "Don't stay up here 'til dark, Levy. I need you to go hunting this evening for some fresh meat."

That made my day. I loved to hunt. It was the adventure, the solitude, maybe just the ability to use a gun that gave me such excitement. Probably because I got a break from working with Jim.

About three hours before dark, I unhooked Jim and we headed to the cabin. I put Jim in the corral, scratched his head, and said, "Wish me luck, my friend."

I ran in the cabin, grabbed my grandfather's old .50-caliber musket, my bag that had extra powder and balls, and headed for the hills. As I was running towards the horizon, I heard my old man yell, "Levy!"

I froze in my tracks and said, "Shit!" I slowly turned and looked back in his direction. I will never forget his smile and wave that day, when he said, "Careful, boy."

I waved back and continued my jog into the hills. I had me a great spot on a creek bank that had a few pools of water below, and with the heat, I knew I would have luck finding something. I brushed myself into a hollowed tree and got comfortable. Put the "Big Fifty" on my knees and muzzled towards the water and cocked the hammer. Cocking the hammer was not the safest thing to do, but I was convinced at the time that the click of the action could be heard for miles. I sat there for a while and was dozing for a few minutes when I heard a rock turn. I opened my eyes and the biggest buck I had ever seen was getting a drink from the pool. I eased my head down to the stock of the Big Fifty and waited for a clean broadside shot. The buck threw his massive antlers upwind and darted straight towards me. It all happened so fast. I could not get the muzzle on the deer for the shot. I mumbled to myself, "What the hell?"

Something scared the deer and must be close, I thought. I just stayed put with the gun at the ready. I could hear hooves on the rocks but couldn't see anything. I thought my heart was going to explode with excitement. Suddenly, out of nowhere, they were there. The light was fading, but there were five magnificent-looking Indians mounted on the hottest, sweatiest, most worn out ponies I had ever seen. The Indians were stealthy quiet as they drank and watered their ponies. I sat there horrified. They scanned their surroundings like weary animals, but different—these men were not afraid, they were confident warriors. I thought to myself, *dear God, please don't let them see me*, as they leaped back on their horses and trotted off.

I dared not move. I don't think I had ever felt that kind of excitement before. My curiosity and fear damn near made me wet myself. I wondered how long I should sit there. My legs and arms violently shook. I told myself to stay still for at least an hour, but it was dark, and I knew my folks would worry if I stayed too long. I waited long enough, to give the Indians time to get further out so they could not hear me move. Suddenly, there were more hooves pounding the ground. My adrenaline shot straight to my heart. I thought for sure this was it. More riders had come to water their horses, and I heard a voice say, "They were definitely here," and another said, "Well, it's too late to track 'em now, let's make camp, men. Dismount!"

Shit, now what do I do? I sat quietly listening to the men talk and build a large fire. Through the light I could make out soldiers in uniforms, with their rifles close by. I figured the men were following the Indians so I would be safe to come out of hiding. I did not move, I just yelled, "Hello in the camp!"

The men jumped and readied their rifles in my direction. One man yelled back at me, "Hold your hands high, and make yourself known, or we'll fire upon you!"

I lowered the hammer on my musket and yelled, "I'm Levy Strickland." I stood up with my musket high over my head and said, "I'm coming out. Please don't shoot!"

One of the men shouted, "There he is!"

Another yelled, "Mister, drop your weapon or carry it butt first!"

I dropped the musket and put my hands in the air and kept walking. They met me about halfway to the fire and someone said, "Hell, it's just a boy!" There must have been eight to ten soldiers surrounding me. They lowered their rifles, and their leader asked, "What're you doing out here all alone?"

"Hunting," I stated.

"Hunting?" he asked.

"Yes, sir. My folks have a place about a mile or so south of here."

The men looked at each other, and one of them said, "Go get your weapon, boy."

I did just that and wondered what the soldiers were mumbling to each other. I retrieved my rifle and walked back to the fire, with all eyes on me. One of the men offered me to have a seat and handed me some jerky. I sat down and chewed the tough, dry meat and began to tell the story of my hunt, as the men stared through me. I finished the jerky and took a small sip of their coffee. One of the men stood up and said, "Son, those Indians you saw are the same ones we've been chasing all over this state."

"Well, they went north from here an hour or so before you got here, and their ponies are pretty much done for," I told the men. "Thank you for the coffee and jerky, but I've got to be going. My folks will be worried sick if I don't head back now."

A soldier said, "Tell us about your family."

"Sir, like I said, we've a small spread just south of here. It's me, my mother, and father, and one no account brother."

The soldiers looked down at the ground and then back into my eyes. The same soldier spoke, "Son, they're gone."

"Gone?" I shouted. "Where could they've gone?"

"Murdered by those same Indians you saw ride north. We just came from your place. Some of my men stayed behind to handle the burying of your family. The Indians killed everyone, including the livestock."

I screamed, "No!" and went into a violent rage.

When I woke up by the fire, my hands and feet were tied.

CHAPTER 2

I looked around me, trying to get my bearings, and I could faintly see the sun on the horizon. My head throbbed painfully, and I was very thirsty. I cleared my throat and said, "Excuse me."

The soldier I had spoke with earlier walked up and said, "Sorry, Levy, you left us no choice but to restrain you."

I asked for some water and to be untied. The soldier put a ladle of water to my lips and said, "Drink, Levy. Now, can you control yourself?"

I gave him my word and he untied me. I asked the man, whose face was bruised and cut, if it was true about my family. He said, "Yes, Levy, I'm sorry, but it's true. My name is Sergeant Jackson, U.S. Cavalry, and we're gonna take care of you. Everything will be fine."

I was crushed and couldn't control my tears. My head hurt badly, and I said, "Well, Mr. Jackson, if you're gonna take care of me like you did last night, no thanks."

Sergeant Jackson said, "Look at my face, Levy."

I asked him if I did that to him. He said, "Yeah, son, but I got off easy. You broke Corporal Everett's nose."

I strangely felt enjoyment knowing I inflicted pain on them. The sergeant asked, "Levy, how old are you?" I told him I was fifteen. The man said, "Shit, we've been beaten by a child."

I told the sergeant I was going home to pay my respects to my family. The sergeant said, "Levy, there's nothing left. The Indians took what they wanted or burned anything that wasn't important to them."

I told the sergeant, "I want my musket and my bag and to be left alone."

The sergeant told me, "Levy, we're going return to the fort with you."

I yelled, "The sombitches we gotta kill are headed north!"

The soldiers all laughed except the sergeant and Corporal Everett. The sergeant said, "Now, Levy, don't make us restrain you again," as he rested his hand on the butt of a shiny Colt revolver.

The horses were saddled. They tied my gun to the side of the saddle, and a burly man said, "Mount up, Levy, and don't give me any shit."

I said, "Yes, sir." Of course, I had no intention of going with them. We mounted and headed south at a slow but deliberate pace. I untied my musket and at the first draw we came to, which was next to a cedar thicket, I slid from the side of the horse, down the draw, and into the cedars just as slick as a snake. I heard one of the soldiers yell to the sergeant, "He's running!"

The sergeant said, "He left the horse and didn't take anything from us. Screw him, he'll come back."

I laughed as I made my way through the brush and thought, *not likely you ass*.

CHAPTER 3

I backtracked, and within an hour I was back at the water hole with nothing but retribution on my mind. The tracks were easy to follow, and I hit them on the jog. I figured they knew the Army would stop chasing them and would never expect a kid on foot. At this point, my life was over anyway as far as I was concerned.

It was almost dark on my second day of running. Eating raw rabbits and whatever else I spotted along the way kept me going. The smell of fire almost caused me to run, but I stopped hard and didn't take another step. I wanted to catch them, but I wasn't sure how to pull it off without being killed. Then it came to me: I could have killed at least one of them when I was hunting, so why not hunt them. I had the wind in my favor, and it was close to dark, so I checked my gun and took my shoes off. I slid through the brush and didn't make a sound. I could hear them, but I couldn't see them. I knew they were close. I quietly climbed up on the side of a large rock and there they were, like sitting ducks.

They had a small fire but were talking and carrying on without a care in the world. I thought, *Levy, this is it.* They had their ponies tied close and looked relaxed when I held my .50-caliber low, cocking the hammer slowly. I took careful aim at the closest Indian's head while he spoke with an Indian to his left. To my good luck, another Indian sat down in from of him. I was pretty sure the ball would travel through the one's head and hit the other in the gut.

I touched the trigger and chaos began. There were two Indians down and three were scrambling to save their own skins. I leapt from the rock and charged into the camp, hitting another Indian with the butt of my gun, breaking the stock into two pieces, but he went down hard and wasn't moving. *That's three*, I thought, as I ran to the head-shot Indian. The other two were on their horses and gone in the blink of an eye. The head-shot Indian was decapitated and no threat. Beside him was my dad's new Winchester rifle. I picked it up and made sure it was loaded. The gut-shot Indian was moaning something. I picked up the tomahawk next to him and buried it into his forehead. The other Indian was coming to but was in bad shape. I was not about to let him get to his feet. I ran a war lance through his middle and watched the life drain from him. I panicked, knowing there were two more somewhere, so I quickly glanced around me and found a good knife and a box of shells. There was also some kind of water canteen made of animal intestine and full of water, so I grabbed it and ran back into the rocks.

I found me a good hide and waited, thinking they might come back. It was two days of sitting in those rocks, not moving at all except to sip water, when I about gave up. That's when I caught movement off to my right. At first, I thought it was a coyote or some animal that caught wind of the death below, but as it crawled to the clearing I saw it was a red animal. An Indian. Great pleasure crossed my face with a smile, and I thought, *that makes four*, as I touched the trigger on my dad's rifle. I levered her and thought, *another one for you, Dad.* The red bastard caught wind of me and sprinted right for me, but I didn't take long— fifty yards is over in a second. I carefully aimed and shot his sorry ass right through the chest. I checked the body and rummaged through the camp once more, finding more cartridges for dad's rifle, a Colt revolver, and I took a pair of moccasins off my dead prey to replace the boots I took off earlier, since I forgot where I put them. I then made me a sling out of some leather that was decorated neatly and put all the ammunition in my bag. The Colt pistol was nice, but I couldn't find any ammunition for it. I decided to take it anyway. I had water, ammo, a knife, and one fine rifle.

The dust had settled, my adrenaline was back to normal, and I was tired. I left their horses and ran south, back towards my folks' place. As I jogged through the country, I found a place to rest. I hid the best I could and slept for what seemed like days. I woke in a panic and thought, *what if their relatives are hunting me?* I went from panicked to pissed and thought to myself, *hunt me you bastards. I'll kill your whole tribe*. I lay there awhile, watching my back trail for any movement. I started walking, slow and cautious like a cat. Then I realized I had nowhere to go, nothing to do, and worst of all, no one to go to. Emotions engulfed me, and I wept for hours. I was tired, sore, and alone. The boy was gone, and the man born, embittered and hard-hearted. I would never cry again and never be afraid again. I welcomed death. Everything I cared for was dead and buried. Time to get the last Indian.

I sat and waited. Chewing on some jerky I took from the Indians' camp, I kept a close eye on the trail behind me. Luck was in my favor. I caught sight of movement, and sure enough, it was my last prey slowly tracking my steps. I became excited and happy, I guess 'cause it gave me a purpose. I watched as the Indian followed my path, and I admired his skills and determination. He was cautious and deliberate. He thought he was hunting me, but I knew the roles were reversed.

I moved very slow, rested my rifle on a rock, and asked myself, *how close should I let him get?* When my dad got the new rifle, we practiced with it a little, and I could hit anything I wanted at a hundred yards or less. *Seventy-five yards, I will drop the hammer.* He was stealth-like, not a big man but very muscular, and he moved like a predator on the trail of his prey. The Indian wore moccasins and a loincloth. The rest of his body was covered in paint or ashes from a fire. He reminded me of a ghost or what I thought a ghost should look like. It was strange to admire a man you were about to kill. I had the rifle up and the hammer cocked. He was following me like he was on a string. I felt myself start to shake while he was about two hundred yards out. The Indian stared right through me, and I panicked. I thought, *that's close enough*, and touched the trigger.

The Indian's leg flew backwards, and he fell, slamming his face on the ground.

I levered the gun and watched. I thought I could see him breathing. There was a large pool of blood coming out of his leg. I slipped down within about thirty yards of him. I was ready for anything. He looked up at me with dark, piercing eyes and said something I couldn't understand. I hope it was something to his maker because whatever he said were his last words. I shot him through the forehead.

I said to myself, "Well, you found me. A lot of good it did you." Something came over me, and I realized they need to know why I'm killing them. I pulled my knife and carved a seven in the Indian's chest. The seven hung on the gate of my family's place and was gonna be our brand if we ever got cattle. I decided to go back to the Indians' campground and carve a seven in a large tree for all who passed by there. I hoped this would let the heathen bastards know I was settling the score.

CHAPTER 4

Walking home, the situation hit me. I had spent several days hunting and killing Indians. This task was done. My family was avenged. Now what? I was tired, hungry, and worst of all, alone.

I made it back to my family's place about dark. I hid myself in the brush and fell asleep. I woke up early, and the sun was just lighting up the horizon. Cold and shaking, I figured winter was not far off. The deer had their antlers, and the mornings were chilly, especially when you were not sure building a fire was a good idea. As the sun got higher in the sky, I started to see the skeleton of what was once my home. There wasn't much left of anything at the cabin, and the barn was mostly some burned posts. The rocks from the fireplace were still there, so I started a small fire to warm up and sat down beside it to check my supplies. I had about ten rifle cartridges, one empty pistol, a knife, and my rifle. I decided the best thing for me to do was to walk to town.

Town was a good eight-hour walk, so I started moving, hoping I would find something to eat along the way. The walk to town passed quickly, but I had no luck finding a meal. I could hear wagons, horses, and people talking as I got closer to town.

The first building was John Jackson's Livery Stable. He was tending to a lame horse as I approached him.

"Hello, Mr. Jackson," I said.

He looked up almost in fear and said, "Damn, Levy, you scared the hell out of me."

I smiled and apologized. I guess I did slip up kind of quietly.

Mr. Jackson said, "Levy, you look like hell. The whole town's been talking about you and your family. The soldiers told us about you running away and everyone just knew you were dead."

"No, sir. I'm alive and hope you could give me a little work to pay for a meal. I haven't had much to eat, and I'm short on supplies."

Mr. Jackson was a friend of my father's, and he said, "Sure, Levy, but first we need to clean you up." We walked to Mr. Jackson's house and were greeted by his wife, Martha. Mrs. Jackson was a large woman, and she instantly grabbed me and hugged me and said, "Poor child."

We sat at the table as Mrs. Jackson poured all the venison stew down me that I could eat. It was delicious. It had soft chunks of meat, potatoes, and carrots. I must have looked like a hungry wolf tearing into my meal when Martha asked me, "Levy, what've you been doing? Where've you been since the tragic loss of your family?"

I scowled as I looked up from my bowl and began telling the story. Mrs. Jackson and Mr. Jackson stared in disbelief at me. When I finished the story, Mr. Jackson said, "Damn, Levy, that's one hell of a story!" Looking at my bloodstained clothes and moccasins, he said again, "Hell of a story!"

Mrs. Jackson found me a shirt and pants to put on while she gave mine a good washing. Mr. Jackson told me times were not good for them, as far as money to pay me, but if I were willing to work, they would give me room and board, which I accepted.

Weeks went by, and I cleaned stalls at the livery stable and occasionally helped Mr. Jackson shoe horses. I would split firewood around town and had managed to save a little money doing odd jobs for the town folks. I had plenty of ammunition, and Mr. Jackson had helped me make a holster and belt for my revolver, which I practiced with as much as time allowed. I would draw the gun and click it on empty cylinders every night and shoot it at least once a week. I was getting very good and was able to draw it quickly and hit a whisky bottle at ten yards or so. I wasn't planning on being a gunfighter or anything like that. I just enjoyed shooting, and it took my mind off of my troubles. I had never had the chance to ride horses much and working at the livery was teaching me all you could want to know about them. Mr. Jackson would buy young horses, and I would ride them until they were gentle, and then he would sell them. He coached me on when to take on the reins and when to use my legs. I learned a lot from him.

I didn't like staying in the Jacksons' house, so I made me a small bunk in the stable. I was warm, dry, and happy. I had made it through the winter and was out shooting in the early spring when I walked back to the livery stable and saw several men standing outside. Mr. Jackson saw me coming up the road and yelled, "Hurry, Levy, we've work to do!"

I jogged up to the livery and saw the town marshal, a couple of deputies, and maybe ten cowboys. Mr. Jackson told me, "Quick, son, saddle up these mounts for the men."

I asked, "What's going on?"

The marshal, Jed Miller, said, "Son, a ranch was just raided north of here by the Indians, and they took a few captives. We're gonna try and find their trail."

I felt my blood run cold and said, "I'm going."

The marshal replied, "No, son, we don't have time to nurse you."

I mumbled, "Son of a bitch," and everyone including the marshal chuckled.

One of the cowboys said, "Hell, Marshal, if the stories are true, that kid has tracked and killed more Indians than anyone here."

The marshal said, "He's not going, and that's final."

I thought to myself, *we'll see about that.*

The lawmen and cowboys left out in a fast lope, and I waited about five minutes and trotted off behind them. I tracked them easily and saw their huge campfire about dark. I stayed back and watched them from a small ridge. I thought it looked like fun down there as they played cards, laughed, and drank from a bottle of whiskey. I sat and watched them most of the night and went to sleep.

The morning came early, and the men were up and broke camp quickly. They saddled their horses and started back to town. I cursed them, and said out loud, "That's why you didn't want me to go." Hell, I didn't need their help for what I wanted to do anyway.

Over the next three days, I tracked the Indians, covering around twenty miles a day. The trail was easy to see, and I had plenty of water and ammunition. The end of the third day, I began to feel like I was getting close, and my adrenaline started rising. I unsaddled my borrowed horse and hid my borrowed saddle under some briars and a couple of trees. I marked the spot with a large, flat rock. I figured if I was Indian hunting, I would be better on foot. I topped my rifle off and filled the cylinder on my pistol, wrapped my canteen around my neck, and headed into the darkness. It was very dark outside, and I was worried I would lose the track, so I stopped and rested until morning.

At first light, I woke up cold and was ready to get moving. I had walked about ten to fifteen miles when I caught the faint smell of smoke in the breeze. I found a good hide and rested until dark. The sun was just going down when I started my stalk. I thought, *Levy, let's go make more stories.*

Everything I did when my family was murdered was questioned and most didn't believe anything that happened. I didn't care. I wasn't doing it for those bastards anyway. I served up a helping of revenge, and I was about to serve up more.

I came upon a deep canyon about midnight or so and could hear a few horses and smell smoke. I could not see a thing but knew I was getting close. I slowly moved to a rock and peered over it and could see the flicker of fire. I lay across the rock and waited till daylight. I was anxious to get to the fighting, but I wanted to see the situation in the daylight before I charged in and got myself killed.

The sun came up directly behind me and gave me my bearings. I had lost track of north, south, east, and west while tracking. There was movement in the camp. I counted five squaws, two young blonde girls, and ten braves. The two young girls were bound together with a pole between them. They looked torn and ragged and couldn't be comfortable. I watched the camp most of the morning as the squaws fed the captives and the bucks lazed around. I was in no hurry to die, so I just watched most of the day to come up with a plan. I was having a tough time figuring what I was going to do when five of the braves jumped on some ponies and headed southeast. I thought to myself, *that's it!*

I jumped to my feet and moved as quickly as I could to intercept them. I didn't get in front of them but fell in behind them as they kept traveling at a fast clip. I thought, *this will work. I'll catch up to them far from this camp, and the bucks at camp won't be able to hear the fight.* I jogged behind the warriors most of the day and could see them some of the time. Night came and I kept running and found them by a small fire. I decided to hit them at first light because I didn't want any of them to escape.

As the sun was coming up, I saw them begin to stir in their camp. One buck started up the fire and the rest huddled around it. I ran through my mind who was first, second, third, and so forth. I was ready. I checked and made sure my revolver was free and cocked the hammer on my rifle. I guessed I was about a hundred yards from the closest Indian, and I put my sights right below his neck, in the middle of his back and touched the trigger. The rifle bucked and the shot knocked him face-first into the fire. I jacked the lever as all hell broke loose and made two more clean kills, but I lost the other two in the brush. I sat there ready and could hear an Indian chanting in the bushes. I raised my rifle in his direction and listened. The chanting continued, and I was getting nervous when the other Indian leapt from the brush on top of me and slashed my arm with his knife as we went to the ground. He was on me like a cat and would have killed me for sure, but my right hand was near my holster, and I was able to bury the revolver in his side and shoot him. I jumped to my feet as the other Indian was running right at me, shooting wildly with an old rifle. I stood my ground as the bullet whizzed by my head, and I shot him through the chest. I believe he died before his body hit the ground. I was excited and felt like the king of the world, then my arm started throbbing. I had forgotten about getting stabbed. I looked down at my left arm, which had a considerable gash in the bicep, and tied my bandana around it tightly. I looked around at my handiwork and found the Indians' ponies. I thought I had better reload my guns first. I loaded everything full of ammunition, cut the hobbles from the tamest horse, and jumped on his back. I looked at the other four ponies and said, "Sorry to leave you like this, but I can't risk you running back to the camp."

I rode off and left them hobbled. I made it back to the remaining Indians and their captives at around dark. I tied the pony securely and made my way in slowly. The girls were still tied to the post, and the squaws and two warriors were still out. I was within fifty yards of the camp before the first brave saw me. I shot him before he said a word, and the squaws and captives started screaming. I levered my rifle and busted the other buck before he knew what was going on. The squaws were screaming and running for the brush, except for one. She was standing by the captive girls with her head held low. I was walking towards her and was about to shoot her, when she looked up and said, "Levy."

"Mom?" I yelled. I dropped my rifle and hugged her. "They told me you were dead."

"No, Son. They killed your father and little brother and took me captive."

"Thank God you're alive," I said.

"No, Son. We'd all be better if I were dead," she said.

I didn't know how to take that statement, because I was still fired up from the fight or maybe just ignorant of the situation, who knows. I asked, "Mom, where are the ponies?" as I cut the two girls loose. I'll never forget the sad, desperate look in those young girls' eyes.

I walked over to a makeshift brush corral and found the two ponies that were left, put my mother on one, and the two girls on the other. I led the two girls up to where I had tied my pony and leapt on his back. We needed to put a lot of ground between us and the dead Indians' camp.

But first there was something I wanted to do. I told my mom and the girls to stay put as I trotted over to where the dead bodies lay. I slid off my stolen pony and took my knife and carved a big seven in both the Indians' chests and mounted back up. I loped up to the girls, causing their horse to spook and jump. Both girls fell to the ground in a thud and started crying. The girls couldn't ride well, and it was going to take too long to get anywhere with them falling off every time the horse stepped wrong. I picked the smallest girl up, she was no more than eight, and put her in front of my mother, and with the mane of the horse and my mom holding her, they looked stable. The next girl, who looked to be about fourteen, had a bit better balance. I pulled her up behind me. I told my mom to stay as close as she could, and we set out as fast as we could without anyone falling off. We rode for a long time in the dark, and my mom yelled, "Levy, we can't go any further!" I protested but knew she was right.

We stopped and dismounted our ponies. My mom and the girls started gathering wood to make a fire. I told them we couldn't build a fire because we were likely being chased by Indians. My mom said, "Levy, no one is chasing us," as she built a large fire.

I sat down on a rock and asked, "Why don't you think we're being followed?"

Mom looked up and said, "Levy, they think you are some kind of warrior spirit, and you have big medicine, avenging the death of your father and brother."

I laughed and said, "I wouldn't bet on it."

My mom said, "No, Son, it's the truth. You are highly respected as a great warrior among them, and you are feared. They talk about the Seven Ranch and how a warrior rose from those ashes and will hunt and kill their braves for many years. That's why they treat me like one of theirs and are afraid of me. They know you are my son."

My mom looked at the ground and said, "They made me take the chief's son as my husband, and I am carrying his child."

I was shocked, and I guess my expression was blank.

My mom said, "It's not like you think. He treated me kinder than any other captive, and it was either fall in with them or be killed."

I told her, "Well, that's then, this is now."

My mom said, "No, Levy, I can't go back to the white people. When they see I'm pregnant with an Indian child, they'll treat me and the child, and possibly you, badly. I'm not going to take a chance on that, Son. Tomorrow morning I'm going back to my husband to raise our child."

My heart sank, and I didn't know if I would ever feel so betrayed or let down again in my life. I looked at her with tears in my eyes and just said, "Okay."

After about an hour of looking into the fire without saying a word, I looked at my mother and said, "If you're choosing your Indian husband and unborn child over me ..."

"That's not what I'm doing!" she screamed. "It's not the child's fault who his father is. He'll never be accepted by the whites."

I spit in the fire and said, "Whatever."

Seeing my mother's grief-stricken face, I asked her to tell me about the chief's son.

"His name is Standing Rock. He left camp about a day before you came in," she said.

I grinned and shook my head and said, "Was he with four other braves?"

My mother said, "Yes. They were going out hunting more captives to raise and try to repopulate their tribe."

I said, "Well, Mom, he won't be back, because I killed all five that rode out of your camp before I came back to get the girls."

My mom shook her head and said, "That can't be true."

I walked off into the brush and said, "Believe what you want. I'll see you in the morning."

CHAPTER 5

I woke up early the next morning. Trying to process the events of the last few days made it impossible to get a good night's sleep. My mind was trying to process the fact that I had killed my mother's husband, and she was now carrying his child. It was a lot to grab on to. I stood by the coals of the fire and looked around the camp. My mother was gone. I thought, *well, at least Mom didn't steal my stolen horses*. I guess I'm a sick person because I chuckled a bit.

The girls slept peacefully, but it was time to get moving. Once the girls were up and ready, I put the youngest in the saddle with me and led the other girl on her pony behind me. I pushed as hard as I could, but there was no way we would make it to town that day. A couple of hours before dark, we pitched camp near a small stream and built a small fire with the wood the girls gathered nearby. The girls hadn't spoken a word all day, which was fine with me, but I told them to stay by the fire, and I would go hunt up some game for a meal. I only walked a short way, and within minutes I had us a doe cooking on the fire. The backstraps would make for a good meal as the fire was burned down perfect for cooking. The girls just sat there looking into space without saying a word. I cooked the venison over the fire and served the girls, who ate as if they had never eaten before. When the girls were finished, I cut me off a slice and sat down by the fire and started to eat.

As I was eating, the oldest girl said, "Thank you, Levy."

I looked up at her and said, "You're welcome, ma'am. You know my name, but I'm afraid I'm at a disadvantage here. I don't know yours."

The girl said, "I'm sorry, Levy, I figured you knew me and my sister. I just figured my father hired you to get us. My name is Ellen Ross, and this is my sister, May."

I said, "Nice to meet you, ma'am. Sorry it's under these circumstances." I told her I wasn't there for her father or pay. "I think I like the hunt and adventure of it."

Ellen said, "Well you are a strange boy then, Levy. Do you know who my father is?"

I said, "No, ma'am."

She laughed and said, "You really are strange. My father owns the largest ranch in the territory. He runs around five thousand head of cattle."

I smiled and said, "Well I guess I do know of your father, but I'm here because I owe the Indians some pain and death, and to be honest, I like hunting them."

Ellen said it again, "You're a strange boy, Levy."

I just laughed and said, "You're probably right."

Ellen said, "Strange or not, you save me and my sister, and I'm so grateful. "Please, Levy, call me Ellie."

I said, "Ma'am, whatever'll make you happy. Let's get some rest."

The girls went to sleep by the fire, and I slipped off into the brush to keep a lookout.

Morning came fast, and I was ready to get those girls out of my hair. We got up and mounted and rode a long way before a word was spoken. "Levy," Ellie said. "May and I want you to know we are not gonna tell anyone about your mother. It's our secret."

I just kept looking straight ahead. I appreciated what they were doing. I protected them and now they were protecting me. I mumbled, "Thank you, Ellie. That's nice of y'all."

"Levy?"

"Yes, Ellie," I replied.

"Those savages haven't used us like you think. They took our clothes off and looked at us, but I don't know why they didn't rape us. I think maybe because we're young, and maybe they didn't want us to hate them."

I said, "Well, Ellie, to be honest, I haven't even thought like that, but now that you mentioned it, you and your sister and your family have a lot to be thankful for."

"Yes, Levy, thanks to you," she replied.

We rode into town and made it to the livery around noon. Mr. Jackson was working hard, and people were filling the streets. I guess we were a sight. Two ragged girls in torn clothes, and a teenage boy riding with two Indian ponies. The whole lot of us looked like we had been to hell and back.

Mr. Jackson looked up and said, "I'll be damned, boy, I thought you had turned into a no-good horse thief, but look at you. Who are your friends?"

I said, "Mr. Jackson, this is Ellen and May Ross."

"Well, I'll be damned, boy, you gone and rescued the Ross girls," Mr. Jackson replied.

The marshal came running across the street as Mr. Jackson called for his wife to come tend to the girls. The marshal asked, "John, what's this?"

Mr. Jackson replied, "Young Levy just brought the Ross girls in."

I stared through the marshal but didn't say a word about how sorry I thought he and his men were.

The marshal looked amazed and said, "Son, I'd like to hear that story."

I said, "Maybe later. I'm tired, and I'm not your son." I walked into the livery and began to clean up. I was washing up and had forgot all about my arm. I walked over to the doc's office, which was on the edge of town, and got myself patched up and then cleaned up. I looked down at my arm when the doc finished and asked what I owed him.

The doc chuckled and said, "No charge, boy. It's on the house."

I smiled and told him thank you. I didn't realize that my last little war had witnesses, and it would change my life forever. It's funny how a decision small or large can change a person's life so quickly and put one on a different path.

I walked back towards the livery, where a crowd had gathered, and heard Mr. Jackson say, "There's the hero!"

I rolled my eyes and several in the crowd laughed. Mr. Jackson said, "Settle down Indian fighter, Martha has you a plate of food over at the house."

I said, "Sounds good, Mr. Jackson." And we headed back to the house.

I stepped up on the porch of the Jacksons' small house, and before I knew it, Mrs. Jackson had me in a bear hug, carrying on like I was her long, lost boy. She even had tears as she looked at me and said, "Thank God you're okay. I was worried sick, young man. Please don't ever leave without telling me again."

She was right. I shouldn't have left without telling anyone. Looking back, I realize now that John and Martha Jackson couldn't have children, and Martha loved me like a son.

I went inside and the Ross girls were sitting in chairs at the table. Mrs. Jackson had helped them clean up and, for the first time, I noticed how pretty they were. Ellie said, "Hi, Levy." May just looked at the table.

I couldn't imagine the fear and crazy adventure they had experienced. I said, "Hello, Ellie," and looked at May, who just stared into the table. I sat down at the table and ate potatoes, carrots, and beef roast that Mrs. Jackson had cooked together. Man, she sure could cook. As I was stuffing my face and enjoying the peace and comfort of being in a safe place, I heard a horse coming at a gallop. I looked up and heard a man yell, "Ellen! May!"

The girls jumped up and ran through the door. The three of them embraced in a big, tearful hug. I have to say, watching the three of them made me happy and a bit jealous. Mrs. Jackson put her hand on my shoulder and said, "Levy, you've done a great thing."

I'll be honest, I was a bit choked up and couldn't muster to say thank you.

The man looked up from the embrace of his daughters and said, "Is that the man?"

Ellie said, "Yes, Pa. That's Levy."

I was shocked he said man. I'm normally son or boy to most people. I stood there as he walked up with May still holding on to him. She was attached to him like a tick, and there was no doubt he was the owner of his girls' hearts. He stuck his hand out and said, "Levy, I'm Frank Ross."

I shook his hand and said, "Levy Strickland."

Frank said, “Sorry about your father, Levy. I knew him. He was a good man.”

I smiled and said, “Yes, sir, he was.”

Frank said, “Levy, I can’t find words to express how grateful I am.” He nodded his head, obviously holding back emotions, and took Ellie and May by the hand and walked them to the livery, where they got on a buggy and headed back to their ranch. As they left, Ellie looked back at me and waved. I smiled and waved back. At the livery, there was still a sizeable crowd. I walked up to several handshakes and pats on the back.

Marshal Miller was still there. He said, “Levy, I’m gonna need you to tell me what happened and the story behind you getting the girls back.”

I said, “Marshal, I found them and got them back. That’s about it.”

The crowd laughed. My stomach was full, and I was feeling wiped out. I looked at Mr. Jackson and asked if he minded if I took a quick nap. Mr. Jackson laughed and said, “Levy, you go rest up, son. You earned it.”

I piled into my bunk and finally slept sound.

CHAPTER 6

I woke up with a start. Mr. Jackson was touching my shoulder and saying my name. I jumped and said, "Shit, how long have I been out?"

Mr. Jackson said, "One full day, but that's not important. Frank Ross is here and wants to see you."

I pulled my boots on and walked out of the livery. Frank was standing by the forge. He took his hand out of his pocket and said, "Afternoon, Levy."

I shook his hand and replied, "Afternoon, sir. I don't know what happened. I've never slept so long."

Frank laughed and said, "I guess you were tired, Levy." Frank was tall, lean, and had black and gray hair sticking out from under his worn but clean cowboy hat. He was a man that just looked like he demanded respect. Frank said, "Levy, I'm no good at small talk, bullshit. I'll make this short. I want you to come work for me."

I told Frank, "Sir, thank you, but I work here for Mr. Jackson."

Frank and Mr. Jackson laughed, and the latter said, "You owe me a beer, Frank. I told you he'd say that."

Frank smiled and said, "I know your situation here, Levy, and I'm offering you a paying job."

"Frank, I'm no cowboy, and all I really know about farming is how to drive a mule."

Frank said, "Levy, I don't give money away to people that don't earn it, and I'm convinced you're a good man. I lost twelve cowboys on that last Indian raid and nearly lost my family. I need good cowboys like any other rancher, but, Levy, I also need good men. I'll supply horses, tack, guns, ammunition, anything you need working for me. My top cowhand makes twenty dollars a month. I'm willing to pay you thirty to be ranch security. All you have to do is be eyes and ears across my ranch and, if necessary, fight for my brand."

I looked at Mr. Jackson and he smiled. I said, "Frank, I think you have a new hand."

Frank said, "Good. Let's get to the barbershop and clean you up. If you're workin' for me, I won't have you lookin' like a cross between a mountain man and a farmer. Go over and get a bath and a haircut. Let old Smiley scrape the peach fuzz off your chin." Frank laughed. "Me and John are getting a drink at the saloon. Come get me when you're done at Smiley's. I'll help you pick out your new duds at the General Store."

As I walked towards the barber, Frank yelled, "Levy, don't tell Smiley anything you don't want the town knowing about!" They laughed and went to the saloon.

I couldn't remember the last time I had bathed or seen a reflection of myself. I walked into the barber and said, "You must be Mr. Smiley."

The man stuck his hand out and said, "Hello, Levy, I'm Freddie. Smiley is just a nickname some of these rounders call me."

I chuckled and said, "Sorry, Freddie. Frank Ross sent me over here to clean up."

I sat in the tub of hot water and scrubbed until the water turned black while Freddie cleaned my worn-out clothes. I stepped out of the tub, and Freddie handed me my clothes. I felt bad about him cleaning them because in a few minutes they were gonna be replaced. When Freddie finished cutting my hair and giving me my first shave, he spun the chair around so I could see myself in the mirror, and I hardly recognized myself.

Freddie said, "There you go, Mr. Strickland, shined up like a new penny."

I said, "Thank you, sir, what do I owe you?"

He said, "Frank took care of it before you came over."

I thought, *how did he know I would take the job?* Then I realized any fool would have taken his offer. I walked over to the saloon and I felt good. I was clean and rested. I walked through the swinging doors and saw Frank and Mr. Jackson at the end of the bar, drinking beer. Frank saw me immediately and said, "Levy, come here, boy." I guess it was the beer, but that was the only time he ever called me boy. He said, "Look, John, I told you there was a man underneath all that dirt, blood, and hair." We all laughed.

Frank said, "Levy, can I buy you a beer?"

I said, "No, thanks, sir."

Frank said, "Good man. Let's go get you some proper work clothes."

We walked into the General Store, and Frank bought me three sets of clothes, a new black hat, and a new pair of boots. I had never worn anything new in my life. I felt guilty for accepting Frank's hospitality, but he wouldn't take no for an answer, and we left out of there carrying armloads of clothes, new winter coats, light jackets, and a rain slicker. If Frank thought I needed it, he bought it. I figured he was a little drunk and showing off a bit, but I think if I were to have turned him down, he would have walloped me. We put all my new gear in Frank's wagon, and I went and told Mrs. Jackson bye. She hugged me and told me how handsome I looked and how proud my folks would be of me. I told her thanks for everything and walked away thinking to myself that maybe my dad and brother would be proud, but who knows about my mom.

I stepped on the wagon and plopped down in the seat as Frank stepped the team off. I asked, "Frank, how long of a ride before we get to your place?"

Frank said we would be on his ranch in about eight hours and another two hours to the house. I thanked him for this generous opportunity he was giving me. Frank never looked at me as he said, "Levy, you don't have children. My children were stolen from me while some of my men ran for their lives and others died. You brought my girls back, and I owe you. Before you say a word about not owing you anything, I feel I do. Besides, you'll earn every penny you get from me. I need a man like you on my ranch. A man not afraid to fight or kill. Levy, men who like to fight and kill are a dime a dozen out here. I believe you're a smart young man who I can trust, and when and if the time comes, you'll use that Colt on your hip for the right reasons. When we get to the ranch, don't discuss your responsibilities or pay with any other of my hands. I expect you to be seen more than heard."

I smiled and said, "Yes, sir."

Frank said, "Levy, I have many acres and many horses and cattle. To go with all this, I have many hands, not all of whom can be trusted. Your job is to watch and build evidence on people that steal from me. The people that steal from me could be a banker, a hand, an Indian, or just a plain ole cattle rustler. The way you took care of my girls, I know you can be trusted with my most valuable property. Can I trust you with everything else?"

I smiled and said, "I won't let you down, sir."

He put his hand on my shoulder and said, "I know, Levy."

We pulled into the ranch about dark. Frank asked, "Are you hungry, Levy?"

I said, "Yes, sir."

He said, "Me too. Let's see what's in the kitchen for grub."

We stepped inside the house and were greeted by Ellie and May. Ellie hugged her dad and shook my hand in a formal greeting kind of way. May stared downward and only nodded when I spoke to her. The house was neat and nice. Nothing fancy, but you would not find a cleaner, neater place in Texas. We sat at the kitchen table and ate beefsteak and potatoes. I don't think I had ever had a better steak in my life. We ate and didn't speak much.

When we finished eating, Frank said, "Levy, I'm tired. Let's get you settled in at the bunkhouse, and we'll talk tomorrow."

We walked outside and a big fellow was unloading supplies. We walked over to the wagon, and Frank said, "Nate, come over here and let me introduce you to Levy."

Nate jumped from the wagon, and I swear I could feel the ground shake. He stuck his hand out and swallowed mine. He shook my hand firm but careful, like he was cautious of his own power.

Frank said, "Levy, this is Nate, my most trusted hand. He looks after things around the house here."

Nate smiled and said, "You're the young man who brought our girls back," and the expression on his face showed true thankfulness.

Frank butted in and said, "Exactly, Nate. Treat him like he's your best friend."

"Yes, sir, Mr. Ross. That I will do," Nate replied.

Frank said, "Good, then show him the bunkhouse," and he turned towards the house. As Frank walked away, he said, "Levy, be ready to ride at seven in the morning, and I'll show you the ranch."

Nate said, "Come on, Levy, let's get you a bunk."

We walked into the bunkhouse. It was dim lit and smelled of cigarette smoke. Nate walked me over to a bunk and said, "This one's yours. Mines right next to you. I'll wake you up at five-thirty, so Mr. Ross won't have to wait on you."

I said, "Thanks, Nate."

He patted me on the back, and I lay down on the bunk and fell right to sleep.

CHAPTER 7

I woke up to Nate shaking my shoulder, saying, "Mr. Levy, time to get up."

Mr. Levy, I thought. It was funny to me. I got out of bed and Nate said, "You and Mr. Ross' horses are waiting up at the house. Go in the kitchen and get you a couple of them biscuits on the table, and there is coffee on the stove. You got a long day today."

I said, "Thanks, Nate," and he just smiled.

As I walked out of the bunkhouse, there were four cowboys on the porch smoking cigarettes and drinking coffee. One said, "Well, lookee here, boys, if it ain't the big Indian fighter." They all chuckled as I turned towards them. I immediately recognized a couple of them from the posse that was playing cards and drinking whiskey instead of chasing Ellie and May's captors. My blood went cold, and I looked at the ass that made the joke, saying, "You got a problem, you son of a bitch?"

Nate grabbed me by the arm and pulled me back. Nate said, "Yes, sir, Mr. Levy, Slim does have a problem, and if he don't learn to show Mr. Levy some respect, it's gonna be a bad problem, because not only am I gonna whip him, he's gonna be looking for a job. Do you understand, Slim?"

Slim said, "Settle down, Nate. I was just having some fun."

Nate said, "Well, no one that matters likes your fun, so keep your comments to yourself."

I figured Slim to be a loudmouth blowhard from the start. Nate looked at me and glanced down to my right hand, which was resting on my Colt pistol. Nate smiled and said, "Levy, don't forget to take your rifle."

I walked back in the bunkhouse and grabbed my rifle and walked back to the porch to find Nate alone. Nate was still smiling, and I asked where everyone went. Nate just said, "Work. What they should have been doing instead of giving you grief."

I smiled and said, "Thanks, Nate, but I can take care of myself."

Nate laughed and said, "Maybe I was taking care of them."

I chuckled and walked towards the house. I knocked on the back door and heard Frank yell, "Come in!" I walked into the kitchen and Frank was at the table eating a biscuit and sipping coffee. Ellie was over by the stove. I had never seen her under good circumstances. I must have been staring at her, because Frank said, "Get you a bite, Levy, and let's go."

Ellie turned and handed me a hot cup of coffee and a biscuit with some kind of sweet jelly on it. My god, she was beautiful. I was embarrassed, and my face was red, I'm sure, but I was able to say, "Thank you, ma'am."

Ellie and Frank both noticed my awkwardness, and Frank started laughing as Ellie said, "Please call me Ellie, Levy."

I said, "Yes, ma'am."

Frank looked up from the table and said, "You ready?"

I said, "Yes, sir," and was never so relieved to leave any place in my life. We walked outside and there were two horses saddled and ready, tied to the railing. Frank untied a big stout-looking sorrel and left a long, lean bay horse that looked like he could run a hole in the wind. I untied him, tied my rifle scabbard to the saddle, patted him on the neck, and whispered, "Easy, little brother" as I stepped up on him.

We stepped the horses up to a trot and went north for over an hour. My seat was sore, and I was getting tired when Frank said, "Let's take a break." I thought to myself, *thank God.*

We pulled up under a tree and took a sip from his canteen. Frank's horse was lathered up pretty good, and the bay I was sitting on had barely broken a sweat.

Frank said, "How do you like your new horse and saddle?"

I said, "A man would be hard to please if a horse and saddle like this couldn't please him."

Frank said, "Well, every good horse deserves a name. What's his name?"

I said, "Well, I guess I will call him Brother."

Frank said, "That's a damn good name, Levy. I like it. What do ya think of the ranch so far?"

I said honestly, "Sir, I haven't noticed much of it. We have been going kinda fast, and I've just been trying to keep up with you."

Frank laughed uncontrollably. When he stopped laughing, he smiled and said, "Levy, you're an honest man, and you've an amazing story, but let's face it, we wouldn't be sitting here talking, if those damn Indians hadn't taken my girls."

"No, sir, I reckon not."

"My girl Ellie has taken a liking to you, son, and I want you to know I believe she could do worse. I hired you to do a job for me that needs to be done, and I don't object to you and Ellie talking and spending time together. Just remember, Levy, if you're anything but a gentleman to my daughter, they'll never find you and probably no one will miss you."

I said, "Frank, I have no plans or intentions of anything with Ellie. I never noticed how handsome she was till this morning."

Frank said, "That may be, son, but my daughter usually gets what she wants, and right now I'm afraid it's you. Give me your word you'll be kind to my daughter and honor me by not taking advantage of the teenage crush she has on you. You're an honorable man, Levy. Aren't you?"

"Well, Frank, I'd no idea any of this was going on, and I'm a bit confused, but I give you my word."

Frank laughed and trotted off again.

We came to a cabin a good three-hour ride from the main house that had a stove, a corral, and a lean-to. Frank said, "It was once a young man's place, but he disappeared. I went to the county and paid the note off for the place. It's used sometimes when weather turns bad or during roundups when it's too far to ride home."

We looked around a bit and kept riding. Frank's ranch was sure a nice place. We rode near twelve hours and saw only a quarter of it. I didn't see much of it while riding with Frank because he traveled a lot of ground fast, and it was all I could do to concentrate on staying on Brother. We rode into the main headquarters about an hour after dark, and I was tired. Nate was standing outside waiting on us.

"Y'all have a good ride?" Nate asked as we rode up.

Frank said, "You bet," and smiled.

Nate said, "Y'all go eat. I'll put your ponies up."

We didn't argue.

We sat at the table, and I ate my fill of beefsteak and potatoes. After I finished, I thanked Frank, Ellie, and May for the meal, then headed to the bunkhouse to get some rest. I walked inside the smoky, dim-lit room to a card game in progress. I walked right past the men and heard a couple of mumbles but couldn't make out what was said. I plopped myself in bed and went right to sleep. I was awakened several times by laughter and snoring.

I woke up the next morning tired. Slim was sitting at the table smoking a cigarette and drinking coffee. I could tell I wasn't welcome and that Slim didn't like me.

I said morning as I passed him and walked outside for some fresh air. I thought about the night Slim played cards and drank whiskey instead of looking for the girls and really didn't care if he liked me or not, because I sure was starting to dislike him. I looked over towards the main house and Frank was sitting in a rocking chair, drinking coffee. He motioned for me to come over and I did.

Frank said, "Mornin', Levy, sleep good?"

I replied, "Yes, sir."

Frank asked, "What you got planned today, Levy?"

I said, "Well, I kinda want to put together some supplies and go back to that cabin we visited yesterday to scout and explore that part of the ranch. I'll be back in a week."

Frank laughed and said, "That's a good idea, Levy. Get started."

I was relieved to get his approval because I didn't know what would happen with

Slim if I stayed, and I was horrified as to what might happen with Ellie if I stayed. I had never been around a girl at all, and to be honest, I was uncomfortable and nervous around her.

Slim was still standing on the porch when Frank yelled at him to saddle my horse. I laughed to myself as Frank said, "Come in, Levy. Let's get Nate to put you some supplies together."

Ellie was in the kitchen when we walked in. Frank asked Nate to put together some beans in a flour sack, salt, pepper, and some bacon. Ellie asked Nate, "Where are you goin', Nate?"

Nate smiled and replied, "Nowhere, Miss Ellie. These supplies are for young Mr. Levy."

Ellie looked at me and said, "Now where are you headed?"

I was kinda upset she was in my business, but I said, "Out for a week or so to explore the ranch."

Nate handed me my bag of supplies, and Frank handed me a box of rifle shells and a box of pistol shells.

Outside, Slim delivered Brother, and I could tell he was less than pleased to be taking care of things for me. I tied my supplies on Brother and stepped up and rode away from the house. I turned back after a bit, and Ellie was standing on the porch, waving. I waved back.

I made it to the cabin by noon and put Brother in the corral. I cleaned the cabin the best I could and put my supplies away. The cabin was a better fit for me than the smoky, old bunkhouse. It felt like home right away.

With Brother put away and my gear taken care of, I grabbed my rifle and headed out on foot.

CHAPTER 8

I liked horses, and they were useful, but I liked sneaking around on foot. I could be quiet and see more on foot, and it was way more comfortable. I walked about a hundred yards from the cabin and found a running creek, so I followed it slow and methodically upstream. I had traveled about three miles or so when I came to a crossing and saw fresh cow tracks and unshod horse tracks. My heart skipped a beat, and I thought, *Indians*. I stayed on the tracks till dark and sat awhile, listening. Occasionally, I thought I could hear talking when the wind blew just right. I walked into the wind, picking up tracks here and there. It wasn't easy in the dark. I could smell smoke from a fire and hear the voices but couldn't see a thing up ahead. I crept as slow and quietly as I could and came to a small canyon. I perched on the rim, and there they were below me. I saw no more than four Indian braves sitting by the fire, talking. It looked like they had ten head of Frank's cattle brushed into the side of the canyon wall as a makeshift corral. My blood ran cold, and I was happy to have found them. I had so much hate built inside me for Indians, that I was almost crazy. I weighed my options and decided there were just four braves, and I would have no problem slipping down to kill them as they slept. I sat for what seemed like an eternity, and three of the braves finally lay down around the fire while one sat up as a guard.

I was about five hundred yards away from them when I started sneaking up on them. I moved down the canyon like a snake, slow and low to the ground. I got within fifty yards, close enough that I could see the one sitting up. He was sound asleep too.

I pulled my rifle up slow and thought, *who's first?* I picked the furthest Indian that was lying down and figured I would work on the hardest shots to the easiest. I touched the trigger on my rifle and heard the bullet thud into the first Indian. I worked the lever and had the sitting Indian nailed before the other two had made it to their feet. I saw the third Indian running towards the horses and shot him. The last Indian had made it to their horses and was galloping away. I turned the cattle loose and went over to the three dead Indians, and I smeared a bloody seven on each of the Indians' ponies, then turned them loose.

I wanted to take evidence to Frank, but the thought of scalping the dead bastards just turned my stomach. I hated Indians, but I guess the thought of cutting their hair from their skull didn't appeal to me. I thought for a while and just did it. As the knife sliced the skin, it made a scraping sound and a tearing noise that I will never forget. I just slipped into a rage and scalped the poor bastards and carved a seven in each of their chests. I tied the scalps to the end of my rifle and made a big circle back to the cabin.

I made it back to the cabin as the sun was coming up and saw smoke in the chimney. Frank's horse was in the corral with Brother. I walked up, and Frank was on the porch leaning back in a chair, sipping coffee.

Frank asked, "Long night?"

"Yes, sir. Went hunting." I held out the rifle with the scalps hanging from the barrel.

Frank said, "You didn't waste any time, did ya?"

I explained what had happened and didn't leave anything out, including the scalping part.

Frank said, "Hell, Levy, you don't have to scalp those boys on my account. Your word is good enough for me."

I said, "Thank you," and walked over to the well and washed the blood from my hands as Frank handed me a cup of coffee.

Frank said, "Ten head of cattle and three dead Indians ain't bad for a day's work."

I looked at Frank and said, "One got away."

Frank laughed and said, "Better luck next time, Levy. I gotta get back. I just brought a couple of steaks for supper last night, and when you didn't come back, I cooked mine. I wrapped yours in a sack. You better cook it today, or it'll likely spoil."

I told Frank thank you, and he mounted up.

Frank said, "Watch yourself, Levy. You may turn from hunter to hunted if you keep killing 'em."

I said, "I hope they do come for me. It'll save me a lot of walking."

Frank laughed and said, "Careful what you wish for." Frank turned to ride off but stopped, turned in his saddle, and asked, "What you gonna do with those scalps?"

I said, "Well, I just took 'em to prove I killed 'em to you. I guess I'll throw 'em away."

Frank said, "No, give 'em to me. I'll take 'em home and show Slim and the boys what kinda man they have been poking at. Maybe they'll learn something before they push you too far."

I said, "Frank, about Slim, can I talk to ya for a minute?"

"What about him?"

I explained how Marshal Miller wouldn't let me go with the posse, and how I followed them and saw what they did. Frank spit and said, "Sombitches. Don't surprise me a bit." Frank rode off, and I thought, *well at least he has a couple of hours to cool down.*

I felt kinda dirty for telling Frank about the marshal and Slim, but I guess my job was to look out for Frank and his family. Slim was trash as far as I could tell.

I built me a small fire and cooked my steak and enjoyed every bite. I took two long logs and made a seven in the front of the cabin and decided it was time for some rest. I looked around and saw a nice rock ledge with a good view of the cabin and hiked up to take me a nice nap. I lay down in the sun and went right to sleep. I don't know how long I had been out, but I woke up and looked down the rock ledge to see several Indians sneaking around the cabin. I sat quietly and watched as they all kinda stopped and stared at the seven in the front yard. I was thinking, *yeah, you bastards, it's me*, as they stood in a trance. I was trying to figure out how to shoot them, when old Slim came a riding into the yard, mad as hell. I guess Slim figured he was gonna come give me a piece of his mind, but he never knew what hit him. The Indians had put four or five arrows in him before he could pick up his reins. Old Slim was lying on the ground bleeding out when I went to work on them Indians. I had four shot before they ever figured out where the shots were coming from. I shot six more before they gave up and ran. I had myself a good fort with the rock ledge, and I made 'em pay. I guess they tracked me back from the creek and was gonna avenge their thieving brothers. I slipped down from my perch and scalped ten Indians, threw Slim on his horse, arrows and all, and saddled Brother to head back to the ranch. I took the scalps once again to prove my story. I didn't want anyone to think I killed old Slim.

Nate was the first to see me ride up, and in just a few minutes the whole ranch was out listening to my story. Most were staring at Slim's bloody corpse and the ten scalps hanging from his saddle.

Frank said, "Levy, Slim rode out of here mad enough to kill you. I guess in a way those Indians saved your life."

I grinned and said, "Maybe so."

Frank said, "Man, you've killed thirteen Indian bucks in two days. Those bastards are gonna be endangered species if they keep running into you."

"I doubt it," I said and started to unsaddle Brother and lead him to the barn. I brushed Brother and turned him out into the corral and turned towards the bunkhouse. Ellie was standing there as I turned. "Hello, Miss Ellie," I said.

She acted mad and said, "It's just Ellie, Levy."

I said, "Sorry, Ellie."

She smiled and said, "You really should be more careful and not take so many chances, Levy."

I smiled and said, "I was kinda careful."

Ellie grabbed me and gave me a hug and said, "Anyway, I'm glad your back."

I said, "Thank you," and walked to the bunkhouse and fell to sleep.

CHAPTER 9

The next morning, I was up before daylight. I saddled Brother up and headed west. The cabin was to the east, and I figured I had the hornets stirred up over there. I was really kind of satisfied when it came to killing Indians, so I rode out of the ranch headquarters as the sun was just over the horizon, and was it a pretty sight. The sun got high enough to be in my eyes, so I stopped under a stand of trees and sat on the ground and looked out across the tall grass. I could hear hoofbeats behind me, so I stood up with my rifle and saw Ellie. She was smiling as she rode up and stepped off her horse.

I said, "Good morning."

She didn't say a word. She walked over and kissed me. I was shocked and embarrassed. I had never been kissed like that before. I said, "Ellie, I can't do this. I promised your dad I wouldn't. I promised him I would not take advantage of you."

She laughed and said, "Well, Levy, I never made such a promise, and I love you." She grabbed me again, and we kissed under the shade.

We sat on the ground holding hands and talked for hours. I was happy and laughing and found that she was what I had been missing in life. I told her she should get back to the house, people would worry about her. "Plus, since I've stirred up the Indians, it really isn't safe for you to be out by yourself."

She smiled and said, "I'm not by myself. Levy, have you ever done it?"

"Done what?" I asked.

"You know, silly, make love."

I must have turned red as a tomato and said, "No, ma'am!"

She smiled and asked, "Would you like to with me?"

I was floored, but before I could even get yes from my mouth, she was kissing me, and we were tangled up on the ground. We made love that day over and over until I just passed out into a coma. I woke up, and she was gone and had left a wildflower in my hat. I smelled the flower and smiled.

I mounted Brother and kept going west until dark. I tied and unsaddled Brother and made a small fire. I ate a bite of jerky and sipped from my canteen. I thought back on the day, and it seemed like a dream. I could still smell her perfume and see her body against mine. Man, she was beautiful. I was a fool in love.

The next morning, I rode awhile further and came across a large herd of cattle grazing in a meadow. There were at least a thousand scattered out across the large green meadow. It was a sight to behold. I looked back on my misfortunes and my recent good luck and couldn't believe the chain of events that put me sitting here on this ridge, looking at the herd of cattle and being in love with the owner's daughter. I turned Brother around and headed back to the ranch.

I got back to the ranch and realized how much nicer the place was without Slim there. Funny how one man can stink up a whole place.

Nate interrupted my thoughts and said, "Come on up the house, Levy, we're about to eat."

I washed my hands and face in the water trough and headed to the house. I sat at the table while Ellie and May brought the food out. Frank walked in and said, "Hey, Levy, you're back. Any scalps or crooked ranch hands today?"

I said, "No, sir, just a peaceful day in the saddle looking over your cattle."

"Thank God for that, young man," he said.

I felt ashamed and guilty for what me and Ellie had done, but when she sat beside me and smiled, I forgot all about my shame. Dinner was good as usual. Nate and I did the dishes and walked over to the bunkhouse and went to bed.

I woke up early, and my curiosity had me wanting to go back to the cabin to see if the Indians' bodies were still there. As I stepped up on Brother, Ellie stepped outside and asked, "Are you headed west today, Levy?"

I said, "No, I gotta go check the cabin for a few days." I could tell she was upset, but I winked at her and blew her a small kiss and kicked Brother into a lope. Man, that horse could travel. We loped for damn near an hour before he even started breathing hard. Frank had given me a real horse. I got within about five miles of the cabin, tied Brother up, unsaddled him, and walked my way in slowly and carefully. I was within eyesight of the cabin and sat awhile. I didn't move until I was sure the coast was clear. I got to the cabin to find the ten bodies I had left on the ground were still there where I left them.

I went back and got Brother and placed him in the corral and made a fire in the stove. I grabbed a blanket and went back to the ridge just in case the Indians came back. I sat there, drifting in and out of sleep most of the night with my rifle across my knees.

I woke up startled as the sun came up and could not believe I had fallen asleep. I watched the place for a while and slipped down to the cabin well after the sun had come up. The Indians had been there that night because the ten bodies on the ground were lined in rocks and Brother had war paint on him. They had him painted up like a war pony with a red seven on each hip. I was a bit nervous and really didn't know what to do. I saddled Brother up and started easing back to the headquarters.

I was less than a mile away from the cabin when I noticed several braves falling in behind me. I thought, *well Levy, this is it.* I gave Brother his head and put the spurs to him. Brother surprised me and the Indians by giving me about five good high bucks, but, man, when he came down on his last buck, he was off like lightning. The Indians let out a couple of war cries and the race was on. I didn't know a horse could run as fast as Brother, but he left those savages and their little ponies like they were going backwards. I pulled way ahead of 'em and stopped. When the Indians got within a couple hundred yards, I shot one and outran them again. I did this two more times, and the fourth time I spun Brother around, the braves turned and went the other way.

Me and old Brother walked the rest of the way home. When we got to headquarters, we must have been a sight. Nate said, "Man, look at ole Brother. He looks like he's been through the wringer and painted up to boot."

Frank walked out and said, "Dammit, Levy, you and your mount look like shit."

I smiled.

Nate asked, "How many did you get?"

"Four."

Frank said, "Levy, you're plum crazy. Nate, come take old Levy's horse."

I said, "No, sir, I got him tonight. He deserves a brushing, a good feeding, and a rub down by the man he saved. I wouldn't be here if it wasn't for this horse."

Frank smiled and said, "Good man."

I loved on that big bay for hours and told him how good he was, and I believe he understood every word. I was just about through with him when Ellie walked in. I told her the story, and she hugged Brother's neck with a tear in her eye and told him, "Thank you for saving my man," then kissed him on the muzzle.

I said, "Whoa there, Ellie, don't go giving away all my kisses."

Ellie smiled and said, "Levy, you just ride west tomorrow, and I'll give you all the kisses you can handle."

I said, "Yes, ma'am," and smiled from ear to ear.

The next morning, I cleaned up in the water trough and headed west to the grove of trees. I sat there for a couple of hours before I saw Ellie on the horizon. She trotted up and without a word, she started tearing at my clothes. We loved each other most of the day and promised each other forever.

I tell you, I wanted her with every breath and loved her like a fairy tale, I reckon. This went on for a while where we would meet at the tree at least once a week. I'm sure Frank knew something was up, but he just ignored it, probably because he knew his girl was happy.

One day, Frank came down to the bunkhouse and said, "Levy, let's go for a ride."

I grabbed old Brother and away we went. We got a mile or so away from the house and he asked, "Levy, how are things with you and Ellie?"

I said, "Frank, we're in love."

Frank looked at the ground and shook his head.

I said, "I'm sorry, Frank. It just kinda happened."

Frank looked up and said, "No, friend, it's me that's sorry. Ellie is a wild child, and I'm afraid you've missed the mark."

I said, "Frank, you're mistaken."

Frank said, "Levy, she's going to school in Boston next week. It's not my idea, but she's been bugging me to go to this school out there for years, and she finally got accepted. I'm sorry, Levy."

I just turned the horse around and headed back to the house. I stepped off Brother at the main house, and Ellie met me on the porch. I asked, "Is it true?"

She replied, "Is what true?"

"You leaving for Boston next week?" I asked.

She said, "Yes, I was waiting for the right time to tell you, Levy."

I said, "No problem," and turned to get a few things for an Indian hunt.

Ellie cried out, "Levy, this is a good opportunity for me. I will come back for Christmas break."

I asked, "How long is this school?"

She said, "Four years."

I said, "Well, Ellie, I'll see you at Christmas then." I stepped up on Brother and headed to the cabin. As I went through the main gate, Frank met me on the trail.

Frank asked, "Where are you headed, Levy?"

I said, "Well, I thought I might go out to the cabin and do some Indian hunting."

Frank smiled and said, "Be careful, son. When you coming back?"

I looked at him and said, "Maybe three weeks." I put old Brother in a lope and got as many miles between me and Ellie as I could. I don't really know what came over me, but I think it was either self-pity or self-destruction. I rode right up to the cabin, not giving a damn if the devil himself was waiting for me. I put Brother in the corral, got my ammunition out of my saddlebags, and went inside the cabin. I walked over to the stove and started a pot of coffee. I sat down at the table and noticed a piece of paper being held down by a rock. I picked it up and read it. My reading was not great but the letter was easy. "Levy, I need to talk to you. Meet me at our old home." It was signed Mom. My jaw hit the floor—two punches in one day. I ate me some jerky and went to bed.

CHAPTER 10

I saddled Brother and headed towards my parents' old place. It was about a two-day ride to my old house, if you took your time and was cautious. I did neither. I pulled up at the old farm right at dark, hoping the whole Indian nation was waiting on me. I was heartsick and really hoping for the worst.

My mom was sitting by a fire in the front yard of where our house used to be. She jumped up and ran over to me and hugged me. "Levy, I've missed you," she said.

I didn't say anything. I stared at the blanket next to the fire. "That's Grey Wolf. He's your half-brother," Mom said.

"Half-brother," I said. The kid was at least two years old. It was hard for me to wrap my head around how much time had passed since we were separated.

Mom said, "Levy, the Indians think you're a Spirit Warrior and that Grey Wolf and I are big medicine because we're kin to you."

I laughed and said, "Well, I don't know about that, but I've thinned out several braves."

"That's why I'm here," Mom said. "They want me to tell you that they want peace with you."

I laughed and said, "Well, I was just gearing up to go on another hunt."

Mom said, "Please, Levy, this is serious. Your brother over there will one day be chief."

I said, "I'm serious, and my brother is buried over there by Dad. Go back and tell those savages to stay off Frank Ross's place and leave his property alone, and I'll leave them alone. I'm gonna ride his place, and if I find so much as a track, I'll hunt them down and kill 'em."

Mom said, “Levy, that’s a deal. They’re afraid of you, and they sent me here to make a treaty with you.”

I said, “Fair enough then.”

I stepped back up on Brother and my mom said, “Levy, drop your hate and be happy with what you have.”

I looked down at her in her braided hair and buckskin clothes and said, “Ma, I don’t have anything but this horse and these guns, and I guess they do make me happy.” I rode off and never looked back.

I rode straight back to the cabin. I didn’t want to see the ranch again until I was sure Ellie was gone. I was tired as hell after more than two full days of riding, so I slept. I figured now that I was at peace with the Indians, I could sleep as long as I wanted without worry.

I hunted around the cabin for about two weeks. I had shot me a young doe and ate her while I was there. I wrestled with my emotions and talked Brother’s ear off. By the time the two weeks were over, me and Brother had determined I was just a rung on a ladder for Miss Ellie, and she was on to the next poor bastard. I saddled Brother up and headed back to headquarters. I had let my guard down when it came to Indians and was riding along without a care in the world. Riding old Brother was therapy for me. When I was on him, it took all my attention and energy to keep him under me, but whatever the reason, it just helped my troubled mind.

Frank and Nate were on me before I even saw them. Frank said, “Morning, Levy. We’re gettin’ worried about you and were trying to find you to make sure you still had your scalp.”

I laughed and took my hat off and said, “I think it’s still there.” Nate chuckled. I said, “Y’all will be happy to know I’ve negotiated a peace treaty for this ranch. The Indians decided they’ll stay off this place and leave your cattle alone.”

I could see the blank stare on their faces and Frank replied, “Treaty? How the hell did you get close enough without killing each other.”

I said, “I’ll tell you if y’all promise not to tell anyone. It’s important to me for people not to know what I am about to tell you.”

Frank and Nate said, “Hell, Levy, your secrets are safe with us. We don’t want you waging war on us.” They both smiled.

I told them when I rescued Ellie and May that I had got my mom back too, but she left in the night because she carried a child by the son of the chief. I let them know it was my mom that came to me about the peace treaty, not the Indians.

Frank said, “Well, I be damned. That’s good news, Levy. Let’s get back and tell the boys. There are parts of this ranch that’ve been off-limits to the cowboys because of the Indian trouble.”

The next year or so was busy. I rode out with the cowboys and watched their backs as they worked. They gathered around five hundred head of cattle that were in parts of the ranch that used to be too dangerous to go. Frank was happy. I was happy. The ranch was a good place to be. May and I had become good friends. We had coffee together in the mornings and would sit on the porch and talk in the evenings. She was a kind soul, quiet and shy to everyone, but she had opened up to me about Ellie, and apparently, Ellie had told her everything we did. I would ask about Ellie from time to time, but May would never say anything about her.

One evening while we were on the porch, joking and carrying on, May asked, "Levy, can you keep a secret?"

I laughed and said, "No, ma'am, I tell Brother everything there is. No secrets between me and Brother."

She giggled and punched me in the arm. She got serious and said, "Promise me, Levy."

I said, "May, you're my best friend in this world. You can tell me anything."

May looked down at the ground and said, "The Indians used me, Ellie somethin' bad."

I said, "I thought they didn't mess with y'all?"

May said, "Ellie lied to you about that. We made a pact to keep our mouths shut about the whole thing because we didn't think any decent man would want us after they found out."

I looked at May and smiled, "Well, May, I don't think any less of you, and your secret is safe with me."

May smiled and said, "Thanks, Levy."

We just sat there in silence for the rest of the evening.

The next morning, we had coffee before I headed out, and we were lighthearted friends again.

Later in the day, I was sitting on a hill, watching some cowboys work with my rifle perched across my lap when Frank rode up and asked, "Want some company?"

I said, "Sir, it's your ranch."

He laughed and said, "That it is." Frank plopped down on the ground, looked out, and said, "Pretty ain't it."

I said, "Yes, sir, very pretty."

Frank was as happy as I had ever seen him, and he thanked me for giving him half his ranch back from the Indians. I chuckled and said, "Well, you're welcome. I really didn't do much, and I haven't hit a lick in a couple of years now."

Frank said, "Levy, you did what an army couldn't do. Thirty bucks a month is the best investment I've ever made on this place. Hell, I checked at the bank and every penny I put in your account is still there. Levy, you got a little over two thousand dollars in the bank."

I said, "Really?"

Frank said, "Yes, sir."

"Well, Frank, I don't guess I've ever needed any money. You've kept me in clothes and ammunition ever since we met."

Frank said, "Money well spent, my boy. I want to talk to you about May. Ever since those damn Indians took her, she's become shy and quiet. She's really made a turn since you two have become friends."

I said, "Hell, Frank, she just needed a friend to talk to."

Frank said, "Yeah, son, but you're definitely what she needed to come out of her slump, and I'm grateful."

"My pleasure, Frank. May is the best friend I got," I replied.

Frank patted me on the back and said, "Levy, it pains me to tell you this, but Ellie is getting married to a pompous banker in Boston. I figured you should know."

I said, "Thanks, Frank, but I'm over all that mess."

Frank said, "Good. I was afraid you wouldn't take the news well. May and I have decided we're not even going to the wedding. Too damn far to travel. I sent the bank over some money to pay for the shindig, but hell, we got work to do around here."

I just grinned, "I reckon so."

That night after supper, I walked out and sat on the porch with May. She was quiet, but she softly said, "Dad tell you about Ellie."

I said, "Yeah, he mentioned it."

She said, "I'm sorry, Levy," and held my hand.

I looked down at her hand, smiled, and said, "Thank you, May, but I'm fine."

Frank walked out and sat down with us. May just kept holding my hand. Frank said, "Levy, there's one more thing I needed to talk to you about, but I'm having a hard time with it."

I said, "Frank, we're all friends here, spit it out."

Frank said, "Well, Levy, that no-account, trashy coward of a marshal, Jed Miller, caught a bullet the other day and is dead."

I smiled and said, "Well, the town is better off for that."

Frank said, "Yeah, but they want to upgrade to you."

May squeezed my hand.

I said, "Hell, Frank, I don't know nothing about the law."

Frank said, "There ain't much to know. If Jed could do it, you damn sure could. The job pays one hundred dollars a month, and they give you a bonus for every arrest and a percentage of the taxes the town collects."

I said, "No kidding."

Frank said, "No, sir. A man could make one hundred and fifty dollars a month pretty damn easy."

By this time, May was squeezing my hand so hard I thought she was trying to break it. I looked down and asked, "Well, Frank, what do you think?"

Frank just laughed and said, "My boy, you got a job here till I die, and from the looks of things, I'm pretty sure May isn't gonna turn loose of you." At that, she let go of my hand. Frank said, "We can talk about your pay if you need more."

I said, "Frank, you pay me too much anyway. You can tell the folks in town I ain't looking for a job, but if their new man ever needs some help with anything, tell him I'm in."

Frank said, "Fair enough." He got up and went inside.

May said, "I was so afraid you were gonna take that job, Levy."

I said, "No, May. I like it here, and someone has to stick around and keep the bandits in check."

She laughed, kissed me on the cheek, and said, "Good night, Levy."

I sat there a while longer, soaking up the day's events, and to tell the truth, I don't think I was ever happier. I guess I had found peace with the Indians, closure with Ellie, and Frank and May were as good friends as a man could want. I hate to admit it, but I was bored with shooting wolves, coyotes, and the occasional black bear. I missed the good old days of hunting Indians, but the Indians hadn't caused any trouble on Frank's ranch, and I wasn't gonna go back on my word with them.

CHAPTER 11

I rode over to my family's old place one day to look around, and it was almost gone. The burned structures were almost all down and rotten, but the grave sites were neatly taken care of with wildflowers growing on them. I was kind of touched that my mom had maintained the graves. I sat down beside them and thought about what May had said about the Indians and how they had used them. I started to think about my mom and how she was right to raise a half-Indian child out here. It would have been difficult in town around white folks. Hell, I disowned her and really had no good reason. I thought she was choosing the Indians over me. The reality was, she was putting her baby first. I thought about how cold-hearted I had been and was truly sorry. I stayed the night there with my guns close by, but no one or nothing came by.

The next morning, I saddled up Brother and headed to the cabin on Frank's ranch. I got to the cabin and found Frank sitting on the porch with a bottle of whiskey. Frank never drank at his house, but from the looks of things, he was sure tying one on today.

As I rode up, Frank said, "Levy, my friend, step down and let's have a drink."

I never drank, but I figured, what the hell. I grabbed a coffee cup, and he poured it full for me. I sipped on the cup while Frank guzzled the bottle. Frank was drunk and out of character, but I guess he needed to cut loose occasionally. Running a ranch like his took a lot of doing. Just keeping the hands paid had to be a nightmare. I respected Frank for what he had and what he was.

Frank said, "Levy, I know Ellie burned you a bit—hell, she hurt me too, acting the way she did. Levy, unless you're blind and ignorant, you got a better deal waiting for you back at the ranch. May is a kinder spirit and a true heart. I know about them girls, I raised 'em."

I said, "Frank, I like May a lot. She's probably the best friend I got next to you."

Frank interrupted. "Being best friends is a damn good place to start for a couple. I reckon you two love each other. You just don't know it yet. I ain't trying to marry you two, but damn, Levy, I ain't gonna live forever, and May is gonna need a good man to keep this place together. I think you two are off to a good start, and damn, she could choose a hell of a lot worse."

I said, "Thank you, Frank. We'll just see what happens, I guess."

Frank said, "Don't be afraid to go out on a limb. You might be missing the chance of a lifetime."

The next day we rode back not saying much. We were both hungover and nauseated from talking philosophy the night before. We had supper that night, and May and I sat on the porch talking as usual. I broke from the small talk and asked May, "Are we just friends, or is there something more you feel for me?"

She smiled and said, "Levy, you sure can be naive. Just because I don't throw myself at you, doesn't mean I'm not attracted to you. I've kissed your cheek, held your hand …" Without warning, she leaned into me and gave me a nice, slow kiss, then asked, "Now what do you think, Levy?"

I smiled and said, "I'm not sure. I may be a bit naive. Can we try that kiss one more time?"

She giggled, leaned into me once again, and her kiss was sweeter than honeysuckle. We embraced for a while afterwards, then she said goodnight, leaving me with a soft petal kiss on the cheek.

I was happy as I could be. Frank was right. Hell, we were best friends, and she was pretty and rich. What the hell was I waiting for?

The next morning, we met in the kitchen and kissed about the time Frank walked in. I was embarrassed and said, "Mr. Ross, I would like your permission to court May."

He replied, "It's Frank, Levy, and you were already given my permission, son. Don't you remember me telling you to? You're gonna have to get a lot smarter if you're gonna run this place."

May laughed and hugged me.

Frank said, "From now on, Levy, you stay right with me. You got a lot of learning to do if I'm gonna trust you with the running of this place. May has a good handle on the finances and business side of things, but there are other things you need to know about, like which end the grass goes in and which end the grass comes out."

May laughed again and told Frank to behave.

May and I were married six months later, and all we had ever done up till our wedding night was kiss and hold each other. I suppose I probably could have had her early if I wanted, but I was kind of scared it would end up like Ellie if we didn't wait. We didn't go anywhere for our honeymoon. Frank and Nate went to the cabin and left us the big house. When May came to me that night, let me tell you, it was worth the wait, and that's all I will say about it. We were best friends, business partners, husband and wife, and as far as I was concerned, no one had it better than me.

Frank was happy too. He pulled May and me into the office one day and said, "I'm seventy years old, that's getting on up there. I want y'all to know I'm proud of our family, and I made a will. I'm giving May a third, Ellie a third, and Levy a third of the ranch. I want you two to buy Ellie out when the time comes. May, you know where I keep the extra money. Just take it and buy her third from her. She has no interest in this place anyway. Now, kids, like I said, I'm getting old. How about a grandchild or two before I die?"

I turned red as a tomato, and May laughed and said, "Well, Pa, I guess I can tell you both at the same time—I'm pregnant."

Frank whooped and yelled while I almost fainted. I think Frank was happier than I was. I was shocked and afraid for the first time in a long time. I had never really felt any responsibilities until that day, but I guess I was as responsible as anyone else I knew, except for Frank, of course.

The next eight months were busy. May was cleaning, painting, rearranging the house. I tried my best to avoid a lot of the chores by watching the cattle graze and riding Brother.

One day, Frank and I went to town for supplies and took a wagon. I had not been to town since I left with Frank around ten years ago. I felt bad for not visiting John and Martha Jackson at the livery. They were kind folks, and I certainly owed them for taking me in. Frank and I talked on the way to town about cow prices, rustling, and Indians. I was glad for the break from baby talk.

We pulled up to the livery, and John was shoeing a horse. He looked up, smiled, and walked over as I stepped off the wagon. He shook my hand and said, "Levy, good to see you. Please go visit with Martha. She talks about you all the time and misses you." I told John I was sorry for staying away. He replied, "Levy, this town has nothing but trouble in it. You've done yourself a favor by staying away."

I smiled and said thank you as I headed to see Martha.

Frank yelled, "I'm gonna go to the barbershop and get old Smiley to clean me up a bit. If I'm not there, I'll be in the saloon having a drink."

I waved and said, "I'll find you."

When I stepped inside John and Martha's home, Martha hugged me till I thought I was gonna break. She was so kind, and there was no doubt she thought of me as her son. We talked for an hour or so, about May and the soon-to-be baby, and she was very excited for sure. I hugged her again and told her I would stop back by before we left town.

I walked by the barbershop and saw that Frank was finishing up. He said, "Right on time, my boy, now you can buy me a drink."

I smiled and said, "You know I don't have any money, Frank."

Frank said, "That's right, don't guess you do."

I told him that I had never held more than a dollar or so in my whole life. Frank said, "Let's go by the bank and introduce you to the banker."

We walked in, and a small man walked right up to Frank and shook his hand and said, "Good to see you, Mr. Ross."

Frank said, "Ted, this is my son-in-law, Levy Strickland."

Ted smiled and shook my hand and said, "Nice to finally meet you, Mr. Strickland."

I smiled and said, "Levy is fine."

Frank said, "Ted, this young man needs to buy me a drink but has no money. Can you fix that?"

Ted laughed and said, "Sure, Mr. Ross, you gentlemen follow me."

We walked into Ted's office and sat down. Ted said, "How much do you need, Levy?"

I had never been in a bank or had any need to go to a bank. I said, "Oh, enough to buy a couple drinks, a meal, and a haircut."

Ted and Frank both laughed. Ted looked in his ledger and walked to a safe and pulled out two hundred dollars. He said, "Please sign the ledger. The number beside your signature is your remaining balance."

I took the pen and said, "Two hundred is too much money."

Frank said, "Shut up, Levy—I'm tired of you never having any money on you."

I looked down to sign my name and saw the balance of $39,800 by my name and said, "That can't be right."

Frank said, "Sure it is. You've never spent a nickel, and with your bonuses and the dowry for marrying my daughter, hell, Levy, you're a well-off gentleman. Besides, I couldn't have my daughter married to a broke cowboy, Indian fighter, could I?"

I didn't know what to say but thank you. We finished up in the bank and walked over towards the saloon. Frank said, "Now you can buy me a drink and pay for your own haircut."

I said, "Frank, you shouldn't have."

He patted me on the back and said, "Son, you're worth every penny and that's final."

We walked in the saloon. I ordered a beer and Frank ordered a whiskey. It felt good to pay for the drinks. I felt like I was worth something. I don't know … it's hard to explain. Money is a powerful thing, and I guess I never felt the power of having any. The saloon was not very crowded. There were about four other people sitting at a table playing cards. We sat and had a couple of drinks and were fixing to leave when one of the men got up from the table and walked over to the bar and stood next to Frank. I thought to myself, *the whole bar is empty, and this guy comes and stands next to us?*

The man ordered a bottle and looked at Frank. He said, "Would you be Frank Ross?"

Frank said, "Yes, sir. This is my son-in-law, Levy. Who are you?"

"The name's Tom Smith, and the other guys at the table are my partners. We're currently out of work and were wondering if you could use any hands?"

Frank replied, "Sorry, Tom, we're full up on the ranch, but I will buy your bottle there. It was nice to meet you."

Tom tipped his hat in thanks and walked away with the bottle.

We were about halfway across the floor to leave when Tom asked, "Levy Strickland?"

I turned and replied, "Yes?"

Tom said, "Damn nice to meet you. I hear you're deadly with those guns, killing Indians and such."

I just replied, "Nice to meet you," and kept walking.

Frank said, "Keep an eye out, Levy. I've a bad feeling about those fellows."

I said, "Yes, sir, me too." We walked over to the General Store and Frank gave them a list of supplies.

The clerk said, "We'll get these things gathered up for you, Mr. Ross."

Frank said, "Take your time. We're gonna go over to the café and eat."

As we walked across town to the café, I saw Tom watching us cross the street. I guess Frank did too, 'cause he said, "That son of a bitch is gonna be trouble."

I agreed and asked, "What do you want to do about it?"

Frank said, "Let's eat."

I laughed. We had our meals, then walked over to the livery to get the wagon. I told John and Martha bye, and Frank invited them out to the ranch to see the baby when it was born. They both smiled and said they would love to come. We rode the wagon over to the General Store and loaded our supplies. Frank hopped up on the wagon with me and kicked the team up to a trot and said, "Let's get home, Levy."

I smiled and said, "Yes, sir. I'm ready."

We had traveled a ways, making good time, when I said, "Frank, I can't help but think those saddle bums from town are following us."

Frank smiled and said, "Me too."

We stopped in a good flat spot and made camp. I built a very large fire, and we stuffed our bedrolls around it, put our hats on one end and boots on the other, smiled at each other, and slipped off in the bushes to wait. The moon was bright, and we had been waiting a couple of hours when I could hear hooves on the ground. I nudged Frank, who had dozed off, and said, "They're here."

We sat and watched as the four men got off their horses, tied them up, and started towards our camp with their rifles in hand. Frank and I took careful aim, and Frank said, "You take the two on the right. I'll get the two on the left."

The men got just outside of the light of the campfire and slowly raised their rifles. That was all Frank needed. He shot first. In just a second or two, we had emptied our rifles, and the four men lay flat on the ground. Frank smiled and said, "Well, I don't guess they'll bushwhack anyone else."

We walked down, and they were all dead. We had cut them to pieces. Frank said, "Levy, go grab those fellows' horses."

I walked over and tied the robbers' horses to the wagon. Frank had laid out all the dead, and I recognized them as Tom Smith and the men from the saloon. Frank looked at me and said, "What a bunch of idiots."

I asked, "Now what?"

Frank said, "Let's get back to the ranch with the supplies."

We traveled all night and pulled up to the ranch about sunup. Frank told Nate the story, and Nate took a couple of hands back to the camp to gather the dead and take them back to the marshal's office. Nate explained the story to the marshal and that was all that was ever said about it.

Those were the first white men I had killed, and I was fine with it. I had no remorse. Funny, every deer or animal I had ever killed, I always felt guilty, but every man so far, I had no bad feelings in my mind, whatsoever. The supplies made it home, Frank and I were safe, nothing else mattered. May was upset that we were in danger, but I think Frank enjoyed the excitement. I know I did.

CHAPTER 12

Within a week of our trip to town, May had us a healthy son. We named him Cole Frank Strickland, after our fathers. Frank was a happy man. He would sit on the porch, rocking with Cole until May would make him hand the baby over.

It was all a blur to me, almost like I was living in a dream. I had a beautiful family, the run of a huge ranch, and more money than I needed. The Indian raid changed my life for sure. I felt guilty for my happiness and my success while the lives of my brother and father were cut short.

Within a few weeks, I got used to the idea of being a dad, and the shock of being one wore off. I took pride in the boy, and he made me smile. I spent most of my time around the house with Cole and May. I really didn't want to miss a second of being a parent. Cole would cry his lungs out with May, Frank, and Nate, but I would take him, and he would stop immediately. I think it made everyone else jealous, except for May. She would laugh and smile and say, "Cole loves his daddy." Life was sure good.

The Indians in the area were pretty much nonexistent. The cavalry had rounded most of them up, and they were on the reservation. I often wondered about my mom and if she was even alive. Squaws were worked hard, and at times it would be hard for a tick to live in the outdoors, let alone a woman. I figured she would be forty-five or so since she was twenty when she had me.

One day, I decided to make a pass around the ranch so I saddled up old Brother. I checked my guns and filled my bags with food and ammunition. I kissed Cole and May, then headed out.

I was about eight hours into my ride when my heart sank. I rode across unshod pony tracks that were headed towards the ranch. It looked like around ten sets of tracks, and I knew it had to be Indians.

I set Brother towards the house. With a loud "heehaw" from me, we were covering ground. All I could think about was May and Cole and all that had happened when I was young. I had to ease up on Brother after a while. He was getting old, and I think I almost killed him. He had white foam all over him and was roaring when he breathed. I felt bad. I got off him and patted his neck and told him I was sorry. I mounted back up, and we took off again at a trot—old or not, Brother could trot all day. It was better at the trot anyway. I could keep my eyes on the tracks. About a half a mile from the house the tracks turned north. I stopped and studied them to find one set continued towards the ranch. I kicked Brother back into a gallop and slid him to a stop, jumping off him at the house with my rifle. I yelled for Frank and May as I ran towards the kitchen door. I hit the door and burst into the house ready for anything, except for what I saw. Frank, May, and Nate were watching an Indian lady hold Cole. I couldn't believe my eyes. It was my mother. She handed Cole to May and hugged me with tears in her eyes. We all sat at the table to hear mom's story about the cavalry rounding up most of the women and children and marching them for miles to the reservation, where many froze or starved to death. She said her son, Grey Wolf, and other warriors escaped the reservation and took her with them. She told about how Grey Wolf was the new chief of what was left of their people, and he had brought her here to be safe from the soldiers and taken care of.

After she was finished, I looked at Frank and May, and they both said, "Of course, Levy."

May handed me Cole and said to my mother, "Come with me, Mrs. Strickland. Let's get you cleaned up and out of those buckskins and into some proper clothing, just in case the cavalry tracks you here."

My mom said, "Thank you, May. Please call me Kate."

May smiled and said, "Come on, Kate, we got a lot to learn about each other."

They went off to clean up and left me, Frank, and Nate sitting with Cole. It was quite a while before anyone spoke. I broke the ice and asked, "Well, Frank, what do you think?"

Frank said, "Levy, she is your mother, and we can't just turn our backs on her. Plus, it'll be nice to have another woman to help out around the house."

Nate smiled and said, "Amen."

Frank smiled too and said, "Well, then, it's settled—she stays."

About an hour later, May opened the door and said, "Gentlemen, may I introduce you to Kate Strickland."

I could not believe it. My mom was pretty and dressed in a powder blue dress, almost identical to the one she wore the day I had last seen her walking away from me to go back to our home. She was smiling and happy. She took Cole from my hands and loved on him. I do believe Frank and Nate were both shocked and amazed at how her transformation took place, being a squaw one minute and the next a respectable-looking lady. It's a good thing she transformed because within thirty minutes the cavalry trotted up in the front yard, wanting to know if we had seen a band of hostile Indians. I did most of the talking and explained I had found their tracks and followed them north until they got into some rocks. The lieutenant thanked me, watered their horses, and they headed north.

When the soldiers left, Frank said, "Well, that's that."

May laughed and hugged my mom. Mom, Ellie, and May went through a lot together when they were kidnapped. May told me later that night that she was happy my mother would be around to help with Cole. I smiled and said, "Yeah, I guess."

I got up early and went for a ride. I wanted to make a small pass around the house and make sure all was safe. I imagined we were safer than ever with my mom at the house.

I got back late that afternoon and found Frank and Mom sitting on the front porch rocking Cole. I sat down with them, and Mom said, "Levy, I need to tell you a few things."

I said, "Well, start telling."

She explained that Grey Wolf, my half-brother, was still full of hate and anger and had vowed an oath to kill me because I had killed his father.

I said, "No, kidding."

Mom said, "You killed him before Grey Wolf was born, and the tribe felt I had put a curse on them and the only way to lift the curse was for Grey Wolf to kill you."

I looked at her and said, "Well, what's keeping him? He knows where I am."

Mom said, "I've been telling him, no, that you had to do what was necessary to survive. I'm afraid without me there, he'll listen to the others and try to lift the curse."

I didn't show it, but I feared for May, Cole, and Frank's safety more than my own. I took Cole and cradled him and said, "Maybe I should go away until this thing is done." I didn't want trouble to come to the ranch because of me.

Frank said, "Nonsense, son, this is where you belong. You're safer here than anywhere."

Mom said, "With the cavalry after 'em, he may never get back to this area."

I asked my mom to describe Grey Wolf to me. She said he favored me a lot, only with darker skin and Indian clothes, and he was taller than the other Indians. I said, "I thought he was still a kid?"

Mom said, "He's fifteen years old and has had a tough life."

I asked, "How does a fifteen-year-old become the chief of a tribe?"

Mom said, "After you killed his father, Grey Wolf was the only heir to the old chief, who died years ago. He only had to prove to be a good hunter and warrior. His size and being related to you made him special in their eyes."

I said, "I sure don't want to kill him, but I'll have to defend myself if he gives me no choice."

Frank said, "Well, hell, maybe he'll never show up around here, but watch yourself, son."

CHAPTER 13

The next year or so seemed uneventful. I chased a few rustlers and practiced with my guns. Frank had an old Sharps .45-120 buffalo gun, and I had been shooting it a bit, practicing at long ranges. I had fun with that old gun, and if I'd had a good rest and could take my time, I was accurate with it out to about six hundred yards. I enjoyed the challenge of guessing the windspeed and hold over with the old rifle. Frank said he had heard of people shooting out to twelve hundred yards with the guns. I had a hard time finding that even possible at that distance.

Cole was doing well. May and Mom had become close friends. I think Frank was kinda sweet on my mom, but Frank hated Indians so much he would never get over Mom being with them, no matter the circumstances. Frank was a hard man, and I guess maybe it was a good thing he never found out that his daughters had been raped by the Indians like my mom had. It was best they never developed their relationship anyway. I think the house would have been weird and small for me if they were a couple. Besides, Frank was in his seventies.

One morning, I was sitting on the porch with Frank, having coffee, when he just dropped his cup and didn't draw another breath. I'll tell you—the pain I felt was the same as the day I lost my own father. Watching the whole ranch mourn was terrible. Cole roamed around the house for weeks asking about PaPa. It was rough, but Frank knew it was coming and had everything taken care of. May took a note out of his safe that gave instructions to go see the lawyer in town, Jack Brown.

I took the letter to town and handed it to Jack, who was visibly distraught over Frank's death. Jack said, "Levy, everything has been planned and taken care of. I will notify Ellie of his passing and send her part of the inheritance."

I shook his hand and said, "Thank you."

As I was walking out the door, Jack said, "Wait, Levy, there's more. Frank told me to read this to you in the event of his death."

As Jack read Frank's words to me, his voice cracked. The letter said: "Well, son, I'm gone. The ranch is all yours and May's. Take care of it and love it. May knows how to keep the place going money-wise, you just do what you do, and be the strength behind the place. Y'all will do well. I have set aside a good sum of money to send Ellie and her banker husband. I have paid Jack to handle the deal, and he has access to the funds. Levy, take care of my daughter and that boy, and I will see you in heaven."

I couldn't help but smile. There would never be another Frank Ross.

People from miles around came to the ranch to pay their last respects to Frank. I saw how many people Frank must have helped or been friends with and was amazed at the turnout.

A week or so after we buried Frank, I was sitting on the porch with Cole and saw a buggy on the horizon. I looked over my shoulder and saw my rifle propped against the house. I always kept it close after Mom told me about Grey Wolf's desire to kill me. The buggy pulled up, and it was Ellie and a fat man in a suit.

Ellie stepped off the buggy and said, "Hello, Levy. That must be my nephew, Cole. This is my husband, Jim."

I shook Jim's hand and said, "Levy Strickland. Nice to meet you." I could tell Jim had never physically worked a day in his life, and he was one heavy man. May came out and screamed with joy and hugged Ellie. Nate took their bags inside, and I took their rig to the barn. I'll admit, I didn't like either of them. I tried to be nice and hide my dislike and distrust.

We were having supper and catching up on old times when I asked Ellie and Jim why they were there. Ellie said, "Well, Levy, we came to visit Father's grave and see Cole."

I said, "I see. Well, it's good y'all came."

I excused myself from the table and was pretty sure I had pissed May off. I roamed around the barn till bedtime and went inside. I found May brushing her hair while Cole slept. May said, "Levy, I don't like them here anymore than you, but they're family, and we should try to be hospitable."

I said, "Yes, ma'am," and went to bed.

The next morning, I got up and went down to breakfast and found Ellie and May talking in the kitchen. I asked Ellie where Jim was. Ellie laughed and said, "Jim usually stays in bed till nine or so."

I just laughed and said, "Okay, then."

May gave me a cold look as I poured my coffee and grabbed a biscuit. I didn't talk much and finished my breakfast while the girls chatted of old times. I excused myself and headed to the barn.

I was saddling my horse when Ellie slipped up behind me without my knowledge. "Going somewhere, Levy?" she asked.

I jumped. "Yeah, old Brother is getting up in years so I'm trying out a few of these new mounts to give him a break."

Ellie said, "We're all getting older, I guess."

I said, "Yes, ma'am."

Ellie said, "I've missed you, Levy."

I said, "Well, thank you, ma'am."

She smiled and asked if I had missed her. I really didn't know how to respond, so I just said, "Things get really busy round here, and I don't think about you much."

She pouted and said, "Well, I was thinking maybe someday we could go for a ride out to the west like we used to do."

I was shocked. She was still bold as ever.

I said, "No, ma'am. There's a renegade Indian out there on the range, and I would advise you to stay here at the house for your safety."

I led the horse out to the yard, stepped up, and rode off to the east. As I passed the house, I saw May on the porch. She waved and blew me a kiss. I smiled, waved back, and kicked the colt into a lope.

I got back to the house later that night and found May already in bed. I got into bed, and May asked how my day went. I said, "Good. Just another day."

May laughed and said, "So every day a married woman throws herself at you?"

I was shocked and asked how she knew. May just laughed and said, "I didn't for sure, but I know my sister, and you were gone a very long time."

I said I was sorry, but thought it was best not to say anything.

May said, "I trust you, Levy, and you don't have to apologize. You don't have to tell me everything."

I asked if she knew how long they were gonna stay. May kissed me and said, "Not long, dear," and we dropped the subject.

The next morning, I got up early, and May asked where I was headed. I told her I was going to the cabin for a few days. May said, "Okay, but watch yourself. There's still your half-brother wanting to kill you."

I said, "Yeah, and your sister trying to screw me." May laughed and threw a pillow at me.

As I mounted up, I thought that May sure was a forgiving angel. If some man was throwing himself at her, I would probably kill him.

My couple of days turned into two weeks. I stayed at the cabin a week, and then rode and camped for another week. I did not see any sign of an Indian the entire trip. I rode back to the ranch to find things hadn't changed. May told me that Jim and Ellie were broke, and the money they had gotten for their part of the ranch was spent to their creditors to keep them out of jail.

I said, "You've got to be kidding me. If that fat bastard thinks he's gonna hang around here and sleep till noon every day, he's another thing coming."

May said, "Now, Levy, she's my sister, and we can't just throw them out."

I was mad and said, "Well, maybe you want me to take your sister out and show her the ranch."

May got mad and said, "No, Levy," and stormed back inside the house.

I think that was the first disagreement May and I ever had. That night we made up and realized it was an impossible situation, and we needed a solution. I really don't think Frank would have wanted me to throw Ellie out, but I am sure he would do something about Jim.

The next morning, I took the Sharps and practiced my long-range shooting from the upstairs balcony. I had targets set out to six hundred yards and a good bench set up. I had practiced here before, and it was a practical spot in case the ranch came under attack. The roar of the Sharps had old Jim up by six o'clock. I decided I would start practicing a few times a week, until either I could hit targets at a thousand yards or Jim and Ellie left. I guess the banker was smarter than me, though, because he started sleeping with earplugs. I didn't know what to do. These two folks were making me unhappy in my own home. Then one day while out riding, it hit me that there could be a lot of worse things going on in my life than two freeloaders camped out in my house. I decided I would just make the best of it and enjoy what I had. I started playing with Cole on the porch, talking with Mom and May, and living just like Ellie and Jim were not there. Life was getting back to normal for me. I never really saw Jim, except for suppertime. I am positive he was the laziest person on earth. Ellie told May that losing everything took the life out of him, and he was not the person she married. I guess old Jim was just living to die, and one day he got tired of waiting. He sat under a live oak tree and shot himself. I felt bad for the old boy and realized he was struggling with being there as much as I was struggling with him being there. In the end, he was thoughtful. He wrote a goodbye note and thanked us for putting up with him. I was thankful he chose to do it outside of the house. I never saw Ellie cry, but May did. We buried old Jim in the cemetery, but not by Frank—those spots were reserved for Ellie and May.

CHAPTER 14

Cole was turning into a good young man. He was smart and strong, a great kid. May and I could not have been happier. Ellie was helping with Cole's education, and things were working out well. I had grown numb to her flirts and lewdness towards me, and to be honest, I guess they kinda made me feel good about myself. Ellie was only a threat to my relationship with May if I let her be, and I wasn't gonna do that.

Times got tough around the country, and cattle thieves took up a lot of my free time. We were losing a lot of cattle to thieves. I had to take a few of our cowboys and make them range security because I couldn't stop the problem by myself. I would rather fight Indians than catch cattle thieves, anyway. I took everyone we caught alive to the town marshal and let him deal with them. I don't know how many we caught or shot protecting ourselves, but it was a lot. I missed the days of hunting Indians and going out by myself. I got so numb to the whole rustler problem that I distanced myself from most of it. May and I had plenty of money, so I just hired guns to protect our ranch. I guess I was getting older and losing some of my venom.

One fall morning, I decided to go out and ride the ranch. I took a good young horse, food, and ammunition. I told May I would see her in a week. I really needed to get away and get some alone time. I rode out to a high ridge and camped. The view was spectacular, and you could see several miles in any direction. I sat there for hours. The next morning, I rode down from the ridge towards the old cabin, and something off to the east caught my attention. I stopped my horse and stared until I saw it again. It was a shiny reflection off a buckle or a gun. I knew something was over there. I decided to trot away from the object and stop in a line of brush about a mile away.

I got to the cover of the brush, jumped off my horse, and stood waiting for about an hour. Just as I started to think I was imagining things, a lone rider stepped out of the cover riding in my direction. He was moving slow and cautious, like a cat sneaking up on its prey. I thought, *there you are you bastard.*

I didn't like my position and hurried to the cabin. I made it to the cabin, put my horse in the corral, and built a fire in the fireplace. Whoever was following me, I wanted them to think I was inside the cabin resting. I hurried up the ledge and waited like I did for the Indians. I sat all evening and all night.

The next day, I thought I would stay till noon before I moved. I figured it to be close to noon, and I was tired, cold, and hungry. I got up and had just started down the ridge when I felt the slap of a bullet hit me high in my left shoulder. The energy of the bullet knocked me down, and I rolled to the ground below the ridge. I lay there still as I could, and I heard a war whoop about a hundred fifty yards to my left. I could hear him running towards me. When I thought, *that's close enough*, I rolled over, drawing my revolver and shooting all in one motion. I hit the young Indian, and he stood there clutching his chest with a puzzled look on his face. I got to my feet as he fell to the ground with a thud. I walked over and kicked his rifle away, as he looked up and said, "I am Grey Wolf. You have killed me, brother."

I looked at his wound, and I had seen people live with worse. I said, "Not today, brother." I plugged his wound with the sleeve of my shirt and made me a sling for my arm with what was left of my shirt, then threw him over the pommel of my saddle. Mounted up, we headed home.

I can't remember a longer, harder ride. My shoulder was hurting something fierce, and trying to keep Grey Wolf across the saddle was tough. We made it to the ranch as dawn was approaching. I yelled from the saddle as loud as I could. "Nate!" I thought, *I'm so weak they will never hear me*, but Nate came out on the porch ready for anything.

Nate grabbed me as I slid from the saddle and said, "I got you, Levy, you're gonna be fine."

I said, "The boy across the saddle is my brother. Help him if you can." I thought he might have been dead—he hadn't made a sound since I shot him.

Nate said, "Yes, sir, but you come first," and he carried me inside.

By now the whole house was jumping. I could hear May in the background just as I blacked out.

I woke up the next morning with May placing a wet towel on my forehead. I looked up, and she smiled at me. I asked how the boy was, and she said Nate was doing everything he could for him and that my mom was there as well. They had taken him in the back, and the doctor had already been out to see to him. They didn't tell anyone else about Grey Wolf, thinking it best to keep it quiet. I told her I thought that was a good idea. We didn't want trouble on our hands. If anyone knew we had a renegade Indian on the ranch, the cavalry would be on our doorstep.

I slept the rest of the day and through till the next morning. I woke and got on my feet, and May met me at the door. She fussed over me and told me I needed to rest, that I had lost a lot of blood. I told her I wanted to see Cole. She yelled for him, and he came running and hugged my leg tight. It's hard to imagine all the fights and hunts I had been on and to realize then that this was my first real injury.

I wanted to see Grey Wolf, so we went to the back room of the house and found him lying quietly under a sheet. They had stripped his clothes off, and he was almost peaceful lying there. I studied his features, and he did look like a darker version of me. My mom hugged me gentle and thanked me for bringing him here. I told her that if he was going to stay, we needed to cut his hair and make him look like a ranch hand, to conceal his identity. Grey Wolf was still unconscious, and Ellie and May wasted no time cleaning him up with a haircut. They had Grey Wolf looking like a cowhand in no time.

I said, "If we are gonna pass him off as a relative, we need a name for him."

Just like that, Grey Wolf the renegade Indian, became Colt Strickland. Colt woke up about a week later, and our mother explained the situation in mixed English and Spanish. It would be a while before Colt would be able to get around. In the meantime, the women worked with his English. I told Mom to make sure he understood that he must drop this desire to kill me, or I would finish what I started. I was not in the habit of turning rattlesnakes loose. He needed to know that if he continued to be a threat to me and my family, I would smother him in the bed he was recovering in. Mom assured me that once he realized I had saved his life, the desire to kill me would stop.

I recovered much quicker than Colt and went back to my normal routines. I even went into town with Nate to pick up supplies. We had made a deal with the bank and the store to pay through drafts, so guys never had to carry money. The marshal noticed my busted shoulder and asked what had happened. I just told him some cow thief got me, and I never saw who or where the shot came from. I guess the reality was we were harboring a fugitive and were outlaws ourselves for doing so.

I visited John and Martha at the livery stable. Martha fed me and Nate like we were long-lost relatives. They were sure good people, and I appreciated all they had done for me.

We finished eating and went by the marshal's office to ask about any recent trouble with Indians or outlaws in the area. The marshal said all was quiet, nothing newsworthy recently. We hopped in the wagon and headed home. On the way back, Nate expressed his concern for the ranch, having an Indian in the house. I was worried about soldiers and the marshal. I hadn't even given thought of the danger to Grey Wolf/Colt himself. I told Nate he was right, and I would think of something.

When we got back, Colt was awake, and I gathered everyone in the living room. I said that Colt and our mother would be moving to the cabin while he continued to recover. I would dress him as a white man and have him provide security on that part of the ranch. He would receive wages, and as soon as his English improved and he was fully recovered, Mom would return to the house. I looked at Colt and asked, "What do you think?" He never replied, just lay there. I figured he was going to be trouble.

The next morning, Nate put Colt in a wagon and covered him with blankets, taking him and my mother to the cabin with all the necessary supplies. I told May I would probably have to kill that bastard one day and that I should have let him die when I shot him. May smiled and kissed me and said, "Levy, you did the right thing, and I'm proud of you."

CHAPTER 15

Within a few months, Colt was up and patrolling the range, and Mom was back playing with Cole. Colt took his job seriously, and I believe he knew that was his only future. We never really spoke to one another. I think he was too prideful to talk to me. It was nice for me to know where he was and that he wasn't trying to kill me.

Life at the ranch grew almost boring, and I practiced shooting a lot. We had hands that did about everything there was to do, and I could only ride around and watch. Ellie had even stopped flirting with me. My life had got flat boring. I had gotten where I could shoot the Sharps very well. I had milk cans out to a thousand yards and hit them more than I missed.

I was sitting up on the balcony practicing one day when I saw about fifteen horsemen coming up the road onto the ranch. They weren't dressed in any uniforms, but they rode in formation. I sat up on the balcony with the big rifle in my lap, and Nate met them as they stopped. The lead man introduced himself as Captain Woodruff and said he and his men were Regulators that protected ranches from theft and looting. They were asking for donations for their cause.

Nate said, "Captain, I just work here. You'll have to talk to Mr. Strickland."

The captain asked, "Well, where is this Strickland fellow?"

I stood up with the big gun in my arms and said, "My friends call me Levy, Captain."

Captain Woodruff looked up, almost embarrassed he hadn't seen me. "Levy? We've heard of you. You'd be the fellow that hunted down the Indians that killed your family."

"Yes, sir, them and others."

Captain Woodruff said, "Yes, sir, boys, this here is the legendary Levy Strickland. He's a real firecracker."

I was getting pissed off with this whole deal. I said, "Captain, I really don't appreciate you riding in here soliciting money from my ranch for protection. We protect ourselves and are good at it. If you look to your right and left, you'll see a dozen or so cowboys with their rifles, and they all know how to use 'em."

Captain Woodruff said, "Mr. Strickland, why don't you just give us five thousand dollars, and we'll be on our way."

I laughed while raising my rifle and said, "Captain, why don't you get the hell off my ranch, before I blow a hole through you big enough to ride through."

Captain Woodruff looked around and saw all my cowboys with raised rifles. He tipped his hat and said, "Yes, sir."

His men slowly turned and started to leave as Woodruff asked, "Are you sure this is the way you want it, Mr. Strickland?"

I exclaimed, "Ride!"

They trotted off slowly, as if to say game on. I yelled at the cowboys to gather up. They all huddled under the balcony. I told four of them to split up and ride in all four directions of the ranch and bring every hand they could find back to the house. I just knew Woodruff and his boys would be back to raid the ranch, and we all needed to be ready.

I sent a teenage hand to town to tell the marshal what just took place. I gathered the family in the kitchen and told them there was going to be trouble, and we had to prepare. Frank had built a huge cellar under the kitchen that was accessible through the pantry door. There were supplies down there and no way a bullet could hit anyone hiding down there. The women agreed that the first sign of trouble they would all go in without hesitation.

I could hear a horse coming first to the kitchen and someone stepped out on the porch. It was my brother, Colt. He said, "Brother, there are several riders surrounding the ranch, and they are in attack formation."

I said, "Thanks, Colt. How many do you think there are?"

Colt estimated thirty to forty. I thought, *damn that Captain Woodruff. He didn't show his whole hand when he dropped in.* I asked Colt, "Brother, would you prefer to fight on horseback or here with us?"

Colt leaped on his horse, but before he could ride off, I said, "Wait," and grabbed some ammunition for him to take. Colt smiled and said, "I have plenty, Brother. Good luck," and he rode out at a trot.

I grabbed the Sharps rifle and sat up on the balcony. May and Cole came and sat with me until dark. I sat there late into the night, waiting, and felt an uncertain feeling come over me. I thought this was not the way to handle this. I stood up and left the big Sharps propped against the wall and went to the office to grab my revolver and my rifle. I told Nate I was gonna go out and see what was going on and that he should get up on the balcony and shoot any man he saw that he didn't recognize.

Nate shook my hand and said, "Be careful, Mr. Levy."

I slipped out the back of the house and kept myself in the shadows of the moon most of the time. I had covered a mile in no time at all. I sat, listened, and smelled for anything that might tell me where Captain Woodruff and his men might be. I heard a limb snap behind me and whirled around with my revolver ready.

"Easy, Brother," Colt said.

I said, "Shit, Colt, you scared me to death."

Colt smiled and said, "I gave you a warning, Brother. You're getting old and slow." Colt told me the main bunch of Captain Woodruff's men were about a half a mile to the west with about ten surrounding the house, keeping watch.

I told him thanks and started walking to the west while Colt followed. We got to the outskirts of their camp and found most of the bunch asleep. Colt slipped up to their horses and knifed the man guarding them, then motioned for me to come up.

I was amazed at how quick and stealthy he could move. I realized then what he meant when he said he gave me warning earlier, and I smiled thinking about the snapping of that limb.

I studied the horses for brands and their tack. There were way too many for us to kill. We cut the horses' lines and let them wander off. Colt and I eased back to cover and decided we should take our chances and cut loose on the men, killing as many as possible, then hustle back to the ranch. Colt eased down close, and I found me a good rock for cover, then we started shooting.

My rifle held seven shots and my pistol six. I was certain most of my shots connected with a person. I know I hit at least ten men and possibly wounded more. I was reloading my guns when Colt came by saying "Come on, Brother, we got 'em good."

When the shooting started, their horses took off and the men panicked, firing blind into the night. We figured we had killed around fifteen men and left the rest on foot. As we were running through the darkness towards the ranch, a sick feeling came over me. That's when I heard gunfire in the distance.

The sun was just coming up as we topped the hill. You could see flames where the house once stood. Everywhere people were shooting. We ran to the barn and started shooting too. We shot men for what seemed like hours until it finally silenced. Captain Woodruff's men were either dead or had retreated.

The house was completely engulfed in fire, and I was horrified at the sight. We all started throwing buckets of water on the house, but it was no use. The house was gone. I feared the worst, and the worst is what we found. Under the kitchen, Ellie, May, Cole, and my Mom were all dead in the cellar. The fire didn't kill them, but the house had collapsed and crushed them.

I guess everyone deals with emotions differently. Some men would have been devastated. Some would have even killed themselves, but I did what I always did since I was a boy—I buried my loved ones and set out to kill the bastards that did this to my family. This time, I had my brother's help.

We picked up the trail and followed Captain Woodruff and the remains of his men. Colt said there was about twenty of them left. We caught up to them about a week after the fire, camped in some rolling hills. They were relaxing, sipping whiskey, and laughing. I was enraged, thinking how men could destroy everything one man has and sit and relax a week later, showing no remorse. Colt slipped around the camp to find a good position. We agreed he wouldn't shoot until I made the first shot. I wanted Captain Woodruff to be the first to die. I saw him stand up and walk to the edge of camp and start to pee. I leveled my Winchester at his head, then thought, *no sir, that's too good for you*. I pulled the rifle down and shot him right in his pecker. He yelled and screamed in pain, then chaos started.

We wiped them out except for a few cowards that ran into the brush like quail. I met Colt in the middle of the camp. He asked, "Brother, what about the others?"

I said, "Get them, Brother."

Colt let out an Indian war whoop that made my skin crawl, and I watched him disappear into the brush.

I walked over to Captain Woodruff and sat down by him, looking at him surrounded by his own blood and obviously in an extreme amount of pain. I asked sarcastically, "You sure this is what you wanted?"

He looked up with hate in his eyes and said, "Finish it!"

I said, "No, sir. You can go to hell when they're ready for you, there's no need to rush it." I told him he deserved torturing for killing everything I ever loved for a measly five thousand dollars. I sat and watched the bastard go to hell and enjoyed every minute of it. It took about an hour for him to pass, by which time Colt had come back to the camp. I asked if it was finished. He just smiled and nodded his head.

We slept there that night amongst the carnage and dead bastards. The next morning, Colt asked if I regretted not paying the men the money. I said, no, that I would never pay someone not to hurt me. Besides, all our cash money was kept at the bank. I didn't have more than five hundred dollars on hand at the house.

I sat back, sipping some of Captain Woodruff's coffee, and realized I had lost track of the number of men I had killed. Grief sat on me, and I realized I had lost my family. I started to cry. Colt sat beside me and said, "Brother, you're a fierce warrior and strong man. Let your emotions out and cry all you need today. Tomorrow, we go back, and you will cry no more." He patted me on the back and walked off.

I thought about what he said and realized I had a ranch to run, men who looked up to me, and families that needed me to survive, so I couldn't go on being a crying boy. I would have to closet my emotions and get the ranch back in order.

CHAPTER 16

The next day, Colt and I gathered horses, supplies, and money out of the raiders' pockets and headed back to the ranch. The raiders had a war chest of about three thousand dollars. When we rode back into the ranch, Nate was there as always to greet me with a smile and a big tear on his cheek. I told Nate to gather every cowboy that was still alive. I wanted to have a meeting in front of the bunkhouse in three hours.

There were about fifty cowboys gathered in front of the bunkhouse as I stepped up to thank them for sticking with me and doing their best to protect my family. I told them we would rebuild the house. The money and horses we gathered from the raiders would be divided evenly amongst them. The men smiled at the thought of about fifty dollars apiece.

We noticed that the horses were marked with a brand of ranch east of us, so we cut out the branded ones and turned the rest loose with the ranch's stock.

The next day, Colt and I headed to the ranch the horses belonged to. The ride was long, and we passed some rough country. We made it to the ranch late evening on the third day's ride. We rode up and were met by two cowboys armed with rifles. The cowboys demanded to know who we were and what we wanted.

I said, "I'm Levy Strickland, and I'm here to talk to whoever runs this place."

The cowboys looked at each other, and one went inside. A few minutes later, the cowboy came back outside with a weathered old man. The old man told us we were welcome and that his name was Nick Wade. Mr. Wade wanted to know what brought us to his place. I told him we had killed a good number of raiders that were mounted on his horses and wondered if he could fill me in on how they came by his property.

Mr. Wade said, "Mr. Strickland, if you step down, we're about to eat supper, and two more mouths to feed is no big deal around here."

We sat down at a big table to steak and beans. There were about ten cowboys eating, and no one spoke but Mr. Wade. He said, "It all started one morning about seven o'clock when Captain Woodruff rode into the yard with about forty men demanding money for protection. I just told him we were a poor ranch just barely scraping by and the only cash we had was in the bank fifty miles from here. Captain Woodruff said he would take horses and cattle in trade for not burning us out. They took fifteen head of horses and a few steers."

I explained my situation and told him if he could spare a few cowboys, they were welcome to ride back with me and Colt to get their horses back.

Mr. Wade said, "Mr. Strickland, you're a good man. You've lost so much and are willing to give back what you fought to get. You're a special kind of fellow."

I said, "Thanks, Mr. Wade, but truth is, I came here to see if you were a part of the outfit that killed my family and burned us out. I came to check you out and if I didn't believe you, I was going to burn you out."

Mr. Wade smiled and said, "Well, I'm glad it didn't come to that, Mr. Strickland."

I smiled and said, "My friends call me Levy."

Mr. Wade sent a few cowboys home with us to retrieve his horses, and they stayed to help us rebuild a modest ranch house. Nate and Colt did most of the work with the help of our own cowboys. Nate was a smart man and had many talents. I think the best thing Nate had was loyalty. I don't believe the Lord had ever made a better human being.

Colt was turning into a handy range boss. He was as good a horseman as there was and cowboying just came naturally. I distanced myself from most of the cowboys and only spoke to Nate and Colt. Some days I didn't speak at all. Colt told me one morning over coffee that he needed to go back to the reservation to pick up some of his property, and that he would be back in a couple of months. I told him it was a bad idea to leave the ranch. On the ranch Colt was a respected cowboy and brother to me. On the reservation he would be Grey Wolf, just another Indian. Colt's mind was made up, though, and I knew there was no stopping him. I offered to buy him whatever he was going back for. Colt laughed at that and said, "Big Brother, money cannot buy everything."

Colt was gone for months. Nate and I had figured him for dead. One day, he just showed up. Colt had the biggest smile on his face, and five Indian squaws with him, which turned out to be his wives. I chuckled and said, "I guess money can't buy the love of five women."

I greeted them all, but none of them spoke any English, so they had no clue what I was saying. Nate spoke Spanish to a degree and was able to communicate when Colt wasn't around. There really wasn't a problem with them. They all did chores and were very helpful. There was one big hurdle we had to get through, though. We had five and a half Comanche Indians living on the ranch, and people hated them worse than anything. Nate proposed that we burn their Indian clothes and dress them all like senoritas. They all spoke pretty good Spanish, and I figured it to be a good plan. I explained the problem to Colt, and he agreed. The squaws had no say in the matter—whatever Colt said, they did.

Watching Colt with his wives brought out the loneliness inside me. I figured things would work out, and they did. After a couple of years of ranching and watching Colt father children, I got a case of wanderlust. I needed to get away. I told Nate and Colt I would be going off for a while, and they both smiled. Nate asked when I would be back, and I told him in less than five years. Colt laughed, but Nate didn't. I was one of the biggest ranchers around, but I didn't want to be a rancher.

The next day, I packed two horses, put my revolver on, and headed north on my adventure.

CHAPTER 17

I stopped in town and got me some spending money and visited with the banker. I told him about my plans of seeing new country. He told me any bank could telegraph him, and he would see that I had money if I needed it through my journey. I shook his hand and said my thanks and walked over to Jack Brown's office. Jack was happy to assist me in whatever I needed. I told him I wanted to make a will, and I wanted it to be legal with no loopholes in it. We wrote out that if something happened to me, the ranch and all my property would be divided in half between Nate and Colt.

With my business taken care of, I headed northwest. I traveled through some flat, open country, stopping at towns for a night or two depending on if they had a saloon or hotel. I made it to the foot of the Rocky Mountains and settled into a small town called Cimarron. They had a nice saloon and hotel.

I would venture out from Cimarron and hunt and explore, and I sure enjoyed the country. You could step out in the morning and see flat land with antelope, head the other direction and see mule deer and elk. I tell you, it was a sportsman's paradise. I didn't shoot anything I didn't eat. I guess I'd had enough killing in my life.

When I was in Cimarron, once people realized who I was, I rarely had to buy a meal or drink.

A reputation is a good thing, but it can be a bad thing as well. Cimarron had some shady characters in it who wouldn't mind building their reputations off poking me into a gunfight. I was a hunter, not a gunfighter, so I packed one morning and headed north to Eagle's Nest.

This was a nice place with a hotel and good food. I stayed several days and didn't make much conversation. I met a young prostitute there, and for the first time in my life, I rented a woman for sex. I liked the girl, and she was as pretty as you could imagine, but when we finished the deal, I tell ya, I never felt so ashamed in my life. I'm not judging men for doing it, and I'm not looking down on women for making a living, but that lifestyle just didn't suit me.

I left Eagle's Nest the next morning and never looked back. I traveled to Denverand enjoyed every second of the trip. When I rode into town, I went straight to the bank. I walked into the bank and there was a beautiful young woman crying and talking to the banker. She abruptly jumped up and headed to the door. We made eye contact, and I tipped my hat and said, "Ma'am." She looked at me with red, swollen eyes, nodded her head, and left.

I walked up to the banker and introduced myself. The banker's name was Eugene Waldrip. He said, "Afternoon, Mr. Strickland. Sorry you had to witness the unpleasant side of my job."

I told him what my banker in Texas had told me about transferring money whenever I needed it. I had left Texas with five hundred dollars, and I still had two hundred. I figured I had been gone approximately one year. Eugene told me he would telegraph the bank and ensure the funds were available, and if I wanted to come back in a couple of hours, everything would be ready. I told him okay and walked down the street to the barbershop. I took a hot bath, got a shave and a haircut. It felt good. I walked over to the café and had an elk steak with potatoes, and it sure was good. I walked over to the bank afterward, and I was treated a lot different. The banker had a spring in his step and a sparkle in his eye. Bankers like money, I suppose.

The whole time I was at the barber and eating, that young woman kept my mind busy. Before Eugene could say much, I said, "Tell me about the young woman that was in here crying."

Eugene said, "That's Catherine Maroney."

I said, "She sure seemed to be in distress."

Eugene said, "Yes. I really shouldn't say anything, but you are a reputable man. Mrs. Maroney's husband and she bought a small place east of here, and he went off looking for gold. Mrs. Maroney's husband has been gone for a year or more, and I fear gone for good."

I asked how much they owed, and Eugene said, "I really can't say." I gave him a glare, and he told me fifteen hundred dollars with penalties and taxes. He asked, "What can I do for you, Mr. Strickland?"

I said, "I need two thousand dollars cash."

Eugene's eyes sparkled as he counted my money. I picked up the money, counted out fifteen hundred of it, and said, "I am Mrs. Maroney's representative. Give me the note on her place with 'paid in full' written across it."

Eugene smiled and said, "Yes, sir, Mr. Strickland."

I put the five hundred in my pocket and folded the bill of sale and put it under my hat. That was a lot of money to spend on someone I didn't know, but hell, I had more money than I needed, and she damn sure needed help.

I walked over to the saloon and bought a round of drinks for the ten or so bums that were there and sipped on my whiskey for probably an hour. I thought Frank must be looking down and smiling. He said a man should be able to buy a drink. I had about ten new best friends in town, not counting the banker.

I walked out about an hour before dark and took my horses to the livery. I paid the liveryman for one night's board and walked over to the hotel. I checked in and the man behind the counter already knew my name. He was a happy fellow and said Mr. Waldrip, the banker, had told him about my good deed. I said, "Yes, sir. She seems like a fine woman."

The hotel clerk smiled and said, "Fine to look at too, Mr. Strickland."

I smiled and told him he would live longer if he minded his own business. I got my key and went to my room and slept like a log until late morning.

The next morn I gathered my things and walked to the lobby of the hotel to find Catherine Maroney waiting for me. She smiled and shook my hand and thanked me. I smiled and told her she was welcome and that I was glad I could help.

I tell you, she was a stunning woman. Hard to believe a man could leave a treasure like that to go search for gold under the ground. Catherine interrupted my thoughts by saying, "Mr. Strickland, can I please cook you supper? It's the least I can do for your kindness."

I smiled and said, "Ma'am, thanks, not necessary," as the hotel clerk listened in on our conversation. I said, "If you'll excuse me, I'll be on my way." I shook her hand and said goodbye.

Catherine said, "If you're ever in town again, stop by, and I will fix you that meal."

I winked at her and said, "Thank you, ma'am," and walked to the livery.

The wind was cold, and my face froze as I rode north out of town. I made it about five miles and couldn't get the sight of Catherine out of my head. I was cold and thought to myself, *Levy, you could be at a warm table eating a home-cooked meal right now.* I turned my horse and headed back.

I rode up to Catherine's place, and she was on the porch in a second welcoming me into her home. She told me to put my horses in the barn, and she would start cooking.

Man, she was something. Quite an amazing-looking woman.

I walked in the house, and she was as busy as a bee cooking and talking. I have to say I sure enjoyed her company. We sat down, and she poured me a cup of coffee. I sipped the coffee while she kept cooking. I had my back to the door, and we were visiting about anything and everything we could think of when the door burst open. Catherine spun around quickly and screamed. I jumped and spun as the first bullet zipped past me, and in a flash, I fired two rounds.

A young man hit the floor dead. Catherine screamed. The first round hit her in the thigh. She was bleeding badly, and I grabbed her and got her to town across the saddle of my horse.

Catherine was losing color as I busted through the door of Doctor Bernard's home and office. I sat there in disbelief as the doctor worked feverishly to stop the bleeding in her leg. As the doctor was bandaging her leg, the marshal came through the door. I didn't hear the marshal ask me any questions until the doc pointed up at him. I looked back at the marshal as he asked again what had happened. I asked the doctor if Catherine would be okay, and Dr. Bernard said, "She has a good chance."

I walked outside with the marshal and told the whole story from beginning to end. The marshal left to go check out my story with the banker. I sat with Catherine until he returned.

Marshal Johnson was a big fellow with pockmarks on his face, and he looked like he could whip a grizzly bear. He told me that the banker and hotel clerk backed up my story, but that my good deed had created a mess in his town. I apologized for the trouble I caused, but that I had no choice in the matter, stating that it was either me or him.

Marshal Johnson said, "That boy was Mrs. Catherine's husband."

I told Marshal Johnson I had figured as much and chalked the thing up as bad luck on my part. Marshal Johnson kinda scowled and said, "Bad luck on everyone's part, I reckon." Marshal Johnson told me not to leave town and to stay out of trouble until he got back in touch with me.

I sat with Catherine on and off for about a week before she could leave Dr. Bernard's office. I paid the doc and thanked him while Catherine got into the buggy I had rented from the livery stable.

I had cleaned her place the best I could and had her husband buried while she recovered from her injury. We drove the buggy and stopped in front of her house. I sat in the seat and apologized for everything and told her I was going to take the buggy back to town and move on. She began to cry and begged me to come back and talk to her before I left. I promised and told her not to worry, that Marshal Johnson had not yet given permission for me to leave town, and I would return to say goodbye.

I took the buggy back to the livery stable and walked over to Marshal Johnson's office. I walked through the door to find him sitting at his desk with his feet propped up, sipping whiskey from a bottle. He smirked and said, "Levy, pull up a chair and have a drink."

I normally didn't drink much, but I felt obligated to sit and sip a few drinks with him. I asked if I was free to leave town. He chuckled and said, "Oh, hell, yeah. I forgot to tell you, the judge said he wanted to forget the whole mess, and the quicker you left town, the better."

I walked back to Catherine's house and knocked on the door. When she said I could enter, I walked in and, man, let me tell you, she didn't look like a woman that nearly died a week ago. She had herself all fixed up and was looking like every young man's dream. Her dark hair was combed up all pretty, and her green eyes, well, they glowed like nothing I had ever seen before in my life. She was a woman from top to bottom.

She asked me to sit down, so I sat at the table—this time facing the door. She said, "I'll trade you stories."

"Pardon me?"

"You have changed my life in a week, and I don't know anything about you."

I told her I really didn't have much to say. She laughed and said, "Fine. I'll start, you listen." She started telling me her life story, which I'd heard most of from the people in town, except for the part about her family, who were poor immigrants and had urged her to marry young. I couldn't take my eyes from her. She was so beautiful that I became entranced with the sound of her musical voice. She met Matt Maroney, her deceased husband, at a church gathering and within months they were married. She told me her marriage was good at first, but they stayed broke, with Matt working as a cowboy at a few ranches and looking for gold in his spare time. They had tried having children, but it never came about, and Matt blamed her for the inability to conceive.

That was the beginning of the end. He made her feel terrible about herself. One day he left and didn't come back.

I said, "Until the night I shot him."

She said, "Levy, you did what anyone would have done to protect themselves, and I believe you saved my life as well."

I looked at the floor and apologized for causing so much trouble. She smiled and said, "You're a kind and humble man."

I smiled and said, "Thanks."

She said, "No, sir, you don't get off that easy. Now, it's your turn to tell me about yourself."

I said, "What the hell. I don't have anywhere to be at the moment."

She hung on every word and seemed fascinated about my life. We decided that I was about fifteen years older than she was, but she wasn't concerned one bit about my age. She told me she was sorry for the tragedy in my life and couldn't imagine how it must have felt to lose May and Cole. I said, "I never talk about the past and try to think on the good things, not the tragedy."

She smiled and said, "Levy, my life here is a mess. Could I travel with you for a while and see how it goes? If you don't like me, and I become trouble, all you have to do is tell me, and I'll come back home."

I told her it sounded like a dream for any man to have a beautiful woman wanting to travel and be with him, but if it was okay with her, I needed to think on it. I could tell she was hurt, and I wished I could have said it a different way, but a beautiful woman can have a lot of power over a man, and I wanted to make the right decision.

I thought I was gonna be strong, but she had me. She stood up and stared through my soul and dropped her dress to the floor. She was picture-perfect and had her body pressed against mine before I could stop her. The next thing I knew, we were making love. She was insatiable, and let me tell you, we made a sport out of making love. I didn't know two people could love the way we did. Needless to say, I gave in, and we put her place up for sale and bought her a good horse.

CHAPTER 18

We traveled from place to place, stayed in hotels, and camped under the stars. We were having a great time, and I never regretted a minute of our time together. We were perfect. The whole time we traveled, I often wondered what was going on at the ranch. One night, as we cuddled under a buffalo robe by the fire, I asked her if she would like to ease down to Texas and see my ranch. She was excited and said, "I thought you would never ask!" I laughed, and we kissed and made love by the fire and started for home the next morning.

The trip home was long and hard, and about five months into the trip, Catherine told me she was pretty sure she was pregnant. I laughed and said, "Well, I guess it was old Matt Maroney's fault after all."

She smiled and said, "I hope you're happy."

I said, "Of course I'm happy."

We stopped in the next town and got married. By the time we got to the ranch, she was close to having the baby, and within a week, I was the proud father of a baby girl. Catherine agreed to name the baby Mayble Strickland. I was happy as anyone, except for Nate, who wanted to name the baby May. I guess we all loved and missed May, but I decided Mayble was close enough to honor the fine woman that touched so many of us.

We were all one big happy family again. Colt was doing well with the ranch. He had made contracts with the very government that once hunted him. He was selling the Army beef and horses. I tell you, he was amazing to watch. He got the best of both races, I believe. He still had four or five wives, and God only knows how many children, but he was a top cowhand and shrewd businessman. Things were so smooth at the ranch that Catherine and I didn't want to disturb things. I liked being kind of an absentee owner, and it would not have been right to come back and start trying to run things. So, Catherine and I left Mayble with Nate one day and went for a ride to pick out our new homesite. We picked a spot with plenty of water and a killer view. Within a year we had a modest home to grow our family in. Catherine was a great partner—we laughed, loved, and had another child together. We named him Samuel Strickland and called him Sam.

I sit here now by this fire and recollect my life, and I am thankful for everything because without one turn in the road, you never get to the next turn. My life has been full. I sit with pen to paper to document my story because I want it told the way I lived it. I don't want my life cheapened or glorified by someone who didn't live it. Catherine and the children wanted my story told, and they are right. My time is drawing near, and I will forever be on the hunt for my future adventure. This is my story.

— Levy Strickland

Made in the USA
Monee, IL
01 February 2021